Florence Marryat

The Risen Dead

Vol. I

Florence Marryat

The Risen Dead
Vol. I

ISBN/EAN: 9783337047689

Printed in Europe, USA, Canada, Australia, Japan

Cover: Foto ©Andreas Hilbeck / pixelio.de

More available books at **www.hansebooks.com**

A Novel

BY

FLORENCE MARRYAT,

AUTHOR OF "LOVE'S CONFLICT," "A SCARLET SIN," ETC., ETC.

IN TWO VOLUMES

VOL. I.

LONDON
SPENCER BLACKETT
35, ST. BRIDE STREET, LUDGATE CIRCUS, E.C.
1891

CONTENTS

CHAPTER I.

CHAPTER II.

CHAPTER III.

CHAPTER IV.

CHAPTER V.

CHAPTER VI.

CHAPTER VII.

CHAPTER VIII.

CHAPTER IX.

CHAPTER X.

CHAPTER XI.

CHAPTER XII.

CHAPTER XIII.

CHAPTER XIV.

THE RISEN DEAD

CHAPTER I.

TOUCH AND GO.

CROWD of foreigners were warmly discussing some subject of interest in a salle à fumer in the "Hôtel des Papilons" in Homburg, and a young Englishman, with a cigar between his lips, was leaning against a pillar and listening to their conversation. It was a hot night in September, and it was late. The gaming-houses had closed, and dark, thunderous-looking clouds, with a warning of rain, had driven the most reckless spirits indoors. There they had broken up into clusters. Some were playing at cards or dominoes; a few were talking over their success at the tables; a

large proportion were smoking, or drinking sullenly by themselves, as they pondered over their losses. But by-and-by an old waiter, apparently well known to all present, commenced to move from one table to another, and chatter and whisper with bated breath and uplifted hands, till one idea seemed to animate every man present.

"Cannot you reason with him, Henri? Will he answer nothing? What does M. Legros say?"

"Mais, messieurs," reiterated Henri, "M. Legros is half beside himself. What to do, he knows not. It is inconceivable, but it is certain. Ce pauvre intends to do himself some injury. And in the 'Papilons,' too. Such a calamity has never happened in the hotel before!"

"I shall not be surprised at anything," ejaculated a German, carelessly. "He has been losing heavily for the last fortnight—we have all seen that—and if he prefers a world where there are no landlords nor hotel bills to Homburg, he has a right to please himself."

" But think of the disgrace, monsieur. It will be our ruin ! " said Henri, wringing his hands.

" Bah ! A fig for your disgrace ! He spent his money royally whilst he had it, and doubtless has paid you double for what he has received. Let the poor fellow have his money's worth for once."

" But has M. Legros expostulated with him ? " inquired another man. " Has he attempted to force the door ? "

At this juncture a little fat man with a bald head, on which the beads of perspiration were standing with anxiety and alarm, was seen making his way between the crowd.

" V'là, m'sieur! " exclaimed the waiter. "Have I expostulated with the gentleman ? Have I attempted to force the door ? " the little man repeated, excitedly. " Messieurs, I give you my solemn word of honour that I have, in reason, done everything. I did not like the look of monsieur when he returned from the tables to-night. It was fixed—stony—immovable. I have seen that look before. I spoke to him, but received no answer. Then he ascended to his room and locked the door. He will neither speak nor open to us, but he has walked the floor for hours, and now all is still, and I fear the worst!"

The men near him burst into a loud peal of derisive laughter.

"Go to, Legros! You have been looking at an empty bottle! What is all this noise about? A man returns to your hotel tired and weary —a little low into the bargain, perhaps — and requires rest and none of your infernal chatter, and you jump to the conclusion that he is a suicide. We ought to duck you for having tried to make fools of us!"

"Gentlemen! gentlemen!" cried the hotel-keeper, in real distress, "this is no laughing matter. Believe me, I know the symptoms of such things better than you do. Monsieur is reckless — not hopeless nor despairing — he has not feeling enough for that—but just indifferent to his life and everything else. I could read it in his face. And he will kill himself if nothing is done to prevent it."

" Break open the door, then, and hand him over to the police!" suggested another listener.

M. Legros's face turned livid at the idea.

" Break open the door!" he ejaculated. " Monsieur cannot consider what he is saying. He might turn the deadly weapon against myself."

" He has reason," interpolated a Frenchman. " I had a friend once — a brave and honest man—who would interfere between two brawlers and separate them, and they turned the knife against him, and he fell pierced to the heart. He had better have left them alone. It is dangerous to meddle with what does not concern one's self."

The young Englishman, who had been listening to all this, suddenly threw away the end of his cigar and stepped into their midst.

" And will you allow the man to die, then, without making an attempt to save his life?" he demanded, with more surprise than anger.

"Will you all sit here and discuss his looks, and deeds, and probable intentions, whilst he may be contemplating suicide upstairs? It is a positive duty for us to do what we can to prevent it."

He spoke fluently and in excellent French, and there was not a man present who did not understand him. And yet not one echoed his sentiments or offered to assist him.

"It is not our business," said the majority, as they slunk back to their cards or dominoes.

"You will do no good by interfering. You had better leave it to M. Legros," replied a chosen few. And the rest looked at him as if he were an impertinent coxcomb, whom they would dearly like to bring to his bearings.

"What! will not one of you respond? Are you utterly indifferent to a fellow-creature's life, or are you afraid of the weapon that may be turned against yourselves?" continued the young Englishman, in a sarcastic voice.

At that word, "afraid," dark brows were sternly lowered, and many an oath was muttered over the insult; but that was all the notice they took of it, and the young man turned to the hotel-keeper.

" M. Legros, what is this gentleman, Englishman or foreigner ? "

" He is an Englishman, the same as monsieur ; one, too, of high family, who knows lords and princes, and——"

"Come ! come ! that does not matter now. Lead me to his room."

" Ah ! monsieur must not be too venturesome. He is really dangerous. Henri peeped into his chamber but a little while since—we have means by which, in moments of danger like the present, we can view the interior of a chambre à coucher— and beheld him, with a white, fixed face, sitting at a table with his pistols before him. But when I rapped respectfully at the door, he ordered me away with an oath, and threatened to settle the first person who attempted to enter his room. So what can we do ? "

" Go to him at once. There is not a moment to be lost. Will you lead the way, monsieur?

You hesitate. Then tell me the number and I
will find it for myself."

"And get a bullet through your head for
your pains," laughed a man, scornfully.

"That is my concern, monsieur, and no one
else's."

"And no loss either, you might have added,"
replied the man, rudely.

The blood rose to the fair face of the Englishman, but this was no moment to pick a quarrel,
so he turned again to the landlord.

"The number, monsieur?"

"If you are resolute," said Legros, deprecatingly, "Henri will conduct you to the end
of the corridor and point out the door. But be
careful, monsieur, I entreat of you. The poor
gentleman is mad. You had better let me send
for the gendarmes to take him away."

"You can do that if you think fit, when I
have failed in my mission," replied the stranger,
as he hurried the old waiter from the salle à
fumer. The comments which followed his departure were not flattering ones.

"A pig-headed Anglais," said one.

"A good thing if his brains are blown out," added another.

"There would be one boaster less in the world!" exclaimed a third man. "Who is he? Where does he come from? He had better wait until the hair has grown upon his chin before he lays down the law for wiser heads than his own."

"Ah! messieurs!" cried Legros, "speak lower, I implore you. Some of his friends may be within hearing. It is a great milord ; a monsieur of the English aristocracy, a son of the Duke Warren. It would be dangerous to affront him. It would ruin my house."

"It appears to me, M. Legros," said one of his customers, who had not hitherto spoken, "that your house is so easily injured, that the only wonder is that it was not in ruins long ago."

Meanwhile, the young Englishman, full of generous warmth and anxiety to save a fellow-creature from destruction, was rushing along the corridor at the top of his speed, towards the fatal bed-chamber.

"V'là, m'sieur, numéro vingt-neuf," said Henri, as he paused at a respectful distance from it, and pointed with his finger.

"Vingt-neuf," repeated the young man to make sure, and then, without hesitation, he walked up to the door and rapped loudly against it with his knuckles.

His interference was rewarded by the sound of a muttered imprecation, and a demand of who was there.

"A friend and a countryman!" replied the young man, cheerily, "and I bring you good news. Please let me in!"

"I don't know you, and I want no news," was the answer. "I beg you will leave me. I wish to be alone."

"Pray open the door," pleaded the fresh young voice. "I have a particular message for you. Let me come in, if only for five minutes."

The man inside the chamber seemed to

hesitate for a few moments, and then he answered gruffly :

"Very well! for five minutes then, though I don't know what on earth you can want with me."

The old waiter slunk into the background as he heard the key turn in the lock, and saw, to his amazement, the younger man admitted to the room. He lingered on the staircase for a moment, half expecting to hear the fatal pistol-shot, with which he believed the desperate stranger would receive his visitor, but as it did not occur, he slipped back into the salle à fumer to relate his experiences. And as he did so, the two men so suddenly brought face to face were standing looking at each other.

"And now what the —— has brought you here ?" demanded the elder. "Do you know that this is an unwarrantable intrusion on my privacy ? What right have you, or any one, to thrust your company on me, uninvited ?"

He was a middle-aged man of about five-and-forty, with gray hair, surmounting a face which bore traces of great physical beauty. He was tall, erect, and well-made, with blue eyes and fair complexion, and a general appearance of vigour that seemed strange in juxtaposition with his prematurely whitened hair. His dress was disordered, his head ruffled, and his whole bearing sullen and defiant; but the younger man's feelings seemed to go forth at once to him, as though he longed to know and own him as a friend. But the manner in which he had been addressed made him feel diffident.

"I know—I feel, sir," he commenced, "that this intrusion must seem impudent to you, but I could not help it. Forgive me. There are rumours passing below that you have been a little unfortunate (as we all are at times) at the tables lately, and I have come to offer myself as your friend. Will you let me be so?"

The elder man laughed sardonically.

"My friend! How do you propose to be that?"

The other got hold of his hand.

"By begging you to pause and consider before

you do anything you may afterwards regret. By asking you to be a little calm and patient, and to confide in me and see if it is not possible that I can help you. To remember that your luck may change again as quickly as it seems to have done now, and that the assistance of a friend may enable you to win back all that you have lost. Only be patient, and do nothing rash."

The elder man wrenched his hand away again, and sank down in a chair, burying his face upon his outstretched arms. The younger one walked deliberately up to the table where the shining revolvers lay ready for their victim, and placed them in the back pocket of his coat. On seeing this, their owner started from his position.

"What makes you do that?" he demanded, furiously. "What right have you to meddle with my property?"

"The right of a friend and fellow-sinner. Have I not already said I wish to be your friend? Let us talk quietly over your affairs this evening, and then if you are still convinced you will be better out of the world than in it, you shall

have your revolvers back again. Isn't that a
fair bargain? You will be able to blow out
your brains just as well to-morrow as to-day—
indeed, I expect better, for your hand is rather
shaky, I perceive, and will be all the steadier
for a night's rest."

The stranger left his seat and walked up to
his side.

"You are rather a remarkable young man,"
he observed, "and rather a plucky one. There
are not many people who would dare to interfere
with my affairs like this. Who and what are
you? I have at least the right to ask the name
of one who constitutes himself my friend whether
I will or no."

"By all means," cried the youth, laughing,
for he felt he had gained his end. "I am not
ashamed of it. My name is Anthony Melstrom,
and I am the second son of Lord Culwarren."

The stranger's white and careworn face became
still more pallid. He staggered slightly as he
reseated himself, and passed his hand in a
puzzled way across his brow.

" Lord Culwarren ! " he repeated. " Culwarren of Gardenholme ? "

" The same, sir," said the young man, eagerly ; " but my father is dead (as perhaps you know), and my brother Philip has the title. We lost our father ten years ago, and my mother has resided almost completely at Gardenholme since. Did you know my father ? "

" How strange, how very strange," murmured his companion, " that his son should lend me a helping hand at such a juncture ! Yes, Mr. Melstrom, I did know Lord Culwarren, but it is now many years ago, indeed before his marriage with your mother, and I have been a wanderer in foreign lands ever since. And so you are actually Culwarren's son ? "

" Only the second, sir—a younger son of no repute whatever, and still less fortune ; but all I have will be gladly at the disposal of my dear father's friend. And may I ask your name in return ? "

" Oh, certainly," replied the stranger, with some confusion, " though the position you found me in to-night makes me rather ashamed to confess it. I am called Fosbrooke—Oliver Fosbrooke."

"Then, Mr. Fosbrooke, I hope you will shake hands with me and say we shall be friends for my father's sake."

"With all my heart, lad," replied Fosbrooke, as he grasped the offered hand warmly. "You've saved my life for the time being, there's no doubt of that, and I suppose I ought to be grateful to you for it; though it would puzzle me (or any man) to say what I have left to live for."

"You must not let our friendship stop here," exclaimed young Melstrom. "You must tell me candidly, Mr. Fosbrooke, what misfortunes have led you to this state of dejection, and let us find the remedy for them. If money can tide the difficulty over, I am sure it can be remedied. Why, if my modest allowance will be of no avail, do you suppose that my brother Culwarren would permit an old friend of our dear father's to——"

"Stop—stop, my dear lad," cried Fosbrooke.

"I can quite understand and appreciate your generous intentions, for I received enough favours from your father in the days gone by, but I cannot avail myself of them. A small loan I may accept at your hands, but my money matters are not so desperate as you may have been led to imagine. My unhappiness — my depression — arises from quite a different cause, and what I was tempted to do to-night—to put an end to thought once and for ever — I have been tempted to do on twenty different occasions, even when my somewhat uncertain coffers were piled with gold."

"But you will never attempt it again," said Anthony, earnestly, "you will promise to try henceforth to look on the brighter side of life— for there is always a brighter side, you know."

"I will promise you one thing, my dear boy," replied Fosbrooke, cheerfully, as he rose and regarded himself in the glass, "and that is to arrange my toilet a little, and try and eat some supper. Do you know that I have not tasted any food for eight-and-forty hours?"

"Let me order them to bring it up here,"

exclaimed Anthony, as he rang the bell. "You mustn't go down amongst that ribald, heartless crew, who have been betting on the probability of your death to-night. We will have a cosy meal and a bottle of champagne together, Fosbrooke, and then you shall tell me all about your troubles, and I will tell you about mine."

"Your troubles?" echoed Fosbrooke, with a derisive laugh, as he regarded the lad's youthful appearance.

"Yes, indeed! I dare say you think I cannot possibly have any, because I do not come of age until next month, but you are mistaken. My very presence here, when I would so much rather be at home, is a real misfortune, as you will acknowledge when you have heard my story."

"Youth, good looks, a pocket full of money, and liberty to travel are not usually considered as misfortunes, my boy."

"No, I suppose not. Yet there are greater troubles than age, or poverty, or an ordinary appearance, Fosbrooke."

"Why, you're quite a philosopher, Melstrom,

and if you go on at this rate, you will be making one of me too. I think you have made a new man of me already. I feel quite glad to think I'm going to sit down to supper, with your bright young face opposite to me, instead of lying stark upon my bedroom floor, with my brains blown out over the carpet. Ah, Anthony! I feel as if I had known you all your life already."

CHAPTER II

ONSIEUR LEGROS, who had never expected another order to issue from numéro vingt-neuf, unless it were for a coffin, was so astonished when he heard that Henri had been told to carry up the best supper and a couple of bottles of the driest champagne that the "Hôtel des Papilons" could afford, for the refreshment of the supposed suicide, that he felt bound to accompany the tray in order to satisfy himself that the marvellous account he had received was true.

"I trust," he commenced, as he timidly looked in at the bedroom door, "that monsieur is served to his satisfaction. If the hour were not so late, and the night so stormy, I should have sent into Homburg for something more recherché; but as

it is " — rubbing his hands deprecatingly " —
" monsieur will be good enough to overlook any
deficiencies."

"Everything seems very nice," replied Fosbrooke, as he glanced at the table.

"Come in, M. Legros," exclaimed Anthony
Melstrom. "I owe you a thousand thanks for
having been terribly mistaken about my friend
Mr. Fosbrooke here. If you had not imagined,
in consequence of his having a raging attack of
toothache and being unable to eat or speak, that
he contemplated putting himself out of the world,
I should never have found out, perhaps, that we
were staying under the same roof."

" Mais, milles pardons," commenced M. Legros,
in dread of Fosbrooke's anger.

"No apologies, monsieur," replied the latter.
" It was a very natural mistake on your part.
Truth to tell, I have felt miserable enough for
anything the last few days, but this fortunate
rencontre with Mr. Melstrom has set me up again,
and after discussing your excellent supper I
expect to be quite myself."

"But he is not a Frenchman, remember," interposed Anthony, "and does not blow out his brains for a finger-ache or a decayed tooth."

"Mais, le mal aux dents—c'est une douleur terrible," exclaimed M. Legros, sympathetically.

"But there's nothing for it like a glass of good champagne," said Melstrom, as the first cork flew, and then Legros and the waiter bowed themselves out of the room, and the newly made friends were left alone.

"It's just as well to put those beggars off the right scent," remarked Melstrom, as he put down his empty glass. "You don't want the whole hotel to be talking of your adventure, Fosbrooke. They've said enough already, I can assure you, and if you take my advice you'll clear out of Homburg as soon as may be."

"I'm afraid I've made an ass of myself," replied Fosbrooke, reflectively, "and I wonder if I have been a greater ass still not to carry out my first intention? When you knocked at my door, Melstrom, and startled me, I had one of my revolvers pointed at my open mouth, and

I can't think why I didn't pull the trigger instead of answering you. Shall I regret my indecision, I wonder? And shall I only have the trouble of going through it all over again, when the dark mood returns upon me?"

"I hope not, Fosbrooke. I hope I have been your deus ex machinâ, and that something more powerful than my own inclination led me to your assistance to-night. But don't talk any more till you have had your supper. Fasting for forty-eight hours is enough to give any man the blues. I believe I should cut my own throat after it."

He lay back in his chair, laughing as he spoke, and his companion took a long survey of him. He was a handsome stripling, tall, and Saxon in feature and appearance, with gray-blue eyes, that could look very sad when a cloud passed over them, but were usually kind and merry.

"You're not a bit like your father, Melstrom," he remarked, presently, as they began their supper. "I suppose you resemble your mother?"

"No, I think not. She is rather dark than

otherwise—so was my father. Culwarren is the image of him."

" Indeed ! Your mother was considered a great beauty, I believe ? I remember reading the accounts of her marriage. Was she not a Miss Fairley, of Oakham ? "

" Yes, Emily Fairley. There were twin sisters, Emily and Ada. Ada married Sir Allan Osprey, and died shortly after, leaving an only daughter, who has always lived with my mother."

" Is she an orphan, then ? "

"Yes. Sir Allan died before his wife. It was the shock, I believe, that killed her. It was a sad business altogether, and my mother felt it very much. But it happened before I can remember."

" Your cousin must be quite like a sister to you, then," said Fosbrooke.

Anthony flushed to the roots of his fair hair, but answered nothing. His companion regarded him in silence and changed the subject.

" Tell me," said the young man, after a pause, " how long you knew my father, Fosbrooke, and why you dropped his acquaintance. I have always heard him spoken of as such a true and constant friend. Miss Paget says he was one of the best men that ever lived."

"Miss Paget! Who is she?"

"I hardly know how to tell you. I suppose most people would call her my mother's companion, but she is much more like her dearest friend and confidante. She has lived with us ever since I can remember, and has been like a second mother to Lily (that's my cousin) and myself. I don't know what we should do without Miss Paget, and Gardenholme would not be itself if she were away."

"You give the lady high praise. Is not Lady Culwarren rather jealous of the influence she has over you?"

"Lady Culwarren! My mother!" exclaimed Anthony Melstrom, colouring again. "Oh, no! She wouldn't care any way, whatever happened to me. Fosbrooke, that is the trouble of my life, I am nothing to my mother."

"My dear fellow, I cannot believe that."

"It is the truth, though. She adores Culwarren. He is a dear fellow, and worthy of her affection, but she might spare a scrap or so for me. The reason I am wandering about the Continent alone now is because she won't have me at Gardenholme."

" Is it possible ? "

" Quite so. You see I am. confiding the history of my troubles to you before I have heard yours. Culwarren is a great book-worm, and is never so happy as when in his library. But I love dogs, and horses, and all field sports, and hardly know what to do with myself in a town. Yet, a twelvemonth ago—only because, I think, she saw I was so happy there—my mother ordered me to leave home for a year's travel. She said I was too rough and boorish, and my mind required cultivation, but — but — I think there were other reasons."

" Won't you confide them to me ? "

" I don't know why I should not. I have no cause to be ashamed of them.   I—I—am fond of my cousin Lily, and I want to marry her—in fact, we are engaged."

" And Lady Culwarren objects to it ? "

" Vehemently, though I cannot say why, for the match seems suitable enough. Lily inherits a small fortune from her parents, and I have the younger son's portion on coming of age. It is not much, but it will be sufficient to marry on. Both the Miss Fairleys had handsome settlements. And my mother loves Lily dearly, and yet she sets her face against her engagement to me. Isn't it strange ? "

" What does the Earl say to it all ? "

" Oh ! he says nothing. He is a very quiet sort of fellow, and not likely to interfere in any quarrel. We have never discussed the subject together."

" And Miss Osprey ? "

" Lily would wait for me a dozen years, and marry me against all opposition. I am sure of that," replied young Melstrom, confidently.

" She writes and tells you so ? "

" No ! that is the worst of it. They won't let her write to me. My mother forbid all correspondence when we parted, and my cousin is naturally bound to obey her. But next month, when I shall be of age, I return to Gardenholme, and then no one will be able to come between us."

"Miss Osprey will be of age also?" inquired Fosbrooke.

"Not for two years, I am sorry to say. She is just nineteen. But if I can only see her, I shall not care, even though my mother should continue to oppose our marriage. But it is hard, isn't it, Fosbrooke, to have one's dearest wishes thwarted for nothing but caprice?"

"Do you wish me to tell you the truth?"

"Why, surely."

"Then I should say that your mother was doing the kindest thing in the world for you by preventing your marriage, and especially to the first woman you've fallen in love with."

"Don't you believe in love, then, and the sacredness of marriage?"

"I believe in passion, Melstrom, and a legal tie that oftener turns into chains of iron than fetters of roses for the unfortunate couples it binds together. You have asked me to tell you the reason that brought me down to the desperate condition in which you found me. I can trace it all back to the treachery, the infidelity, the weak faith of a woman."

"A woman!" echoed Anthony, starting.

Fosbrooke smiled.

"Yes, my boy, a woman. I suppose you think because my hair is gray, and I have reached middle age, that my blood must run cold, and I have done with all the weaknesses and temptations of youth. But let that pass. The woman I allude to is not in Homburg—is not, indeed, in this world; she passed out of it many years ago. Were it not so, I do not think I could trust myself to speak of her — even now. She was very beautiful, Anthony, and she was my wife in the eyes of God and man. But she did not love me enough to have complete faith in me. She married me secretly—there is no need to tell you why—but when those who were interested in separating us brought falsehoods to her against my character, and said I had legal ties existing which prevented her being my lawful wife, she believed them instead of me, and left me without any clue to her discovery, and died of the broken heart she had brought upon herself. And when she did that, my boy, she broke mine too."

"She must have loved you very much," said Anthony Melstrom, gently.

"She did; but the more I believed in her affection for me, the greater my remorse became. It is remorse that has carved out my life and made me what I am. The remembrance of her want of faith in my honour had no power to quell that, though it has turned me against the whole sex for her sake. There is but one way to live happy or content, Melstrom. Avoid women as you would a pestilence. Abjure love and marriage; they are only cheats to lure men to their destruction—mirages in the desert of life, which promise satisfaction, but vanish as you approach close to them. Keep to yourself, and if not happy, you can at least be free. Give up your liberty and you become a slave, without any compensation."

"Fosbrooke, you are a misanthrope!" exclaimed his companion; "you view the world
through the memory of your own disappointment.
You don't know what it is to be doubly happy
in the presence of one you love."

"Don't I, my boy?" cried Fosbrooke, as he
drained another glass of champagne. "That's all
you know about it. Do you think there is no
happiness in this world without making love?
That's a boy's creed. Have you never heard
of the land of Bohemia—the world of wit, and
language, and song; where the care is lightest,
and the talk is brightest, and we turn the night
into the day, or the day into the night, just as
it may please our unfettered spirits to do? That
is *my* world, Anthony—the kingdom I have
possessed now for over twenty years, in which
I shall reign till I die. There are no women
there, my friend, or not, at all events, in the
set to which I belong; and if they do enter, it
is on sufferance, and we neither love them nor
hate them sufficiently to make our hearts ache.
That is the place to live and die in—the Land

of Bohemia. Let us drink to it in a flowing bumper."

"And yet, beautiful and pleasant as you assert it to be, Fosbrooke, you did not seem to show much reluctance at leaving it just now. How is that?" demanded Melstrom.

For a moment Fosbrooke looked puzzled what to reply.

"Well, you see, my dear Anthony, the glass will fall sometimes, and even in Bohemia does not always point at 'Fair.' Besides, I have none of my bons camarades with me in Homburg, and I must confess that I have been drinking too much lately—all from want of companionship—and playing too high. When I am alone for a few days, old memories come pouring back upon me in such a flood, that I am not always master of myself. And then I have lost confoundedly—been completely cleared out, in fact, and I shall have to raise the wind till my remittances fall due again. So, taking one thing and another into consideration, I thought I might as well make a bolt of it for the other side. And I'm not quite clear yet whether I'm obliged to you for spoiling my little game."

"Oh yes, you are," exclaimed the younger man; "and you will be still more so to-morrow. Look here, Fosbrooke, I have a proposal to make to you. Let us travel on together. I have more ammunition than I need to carry on the war, and can easily be your banker till your remittances arrive. And it will be a real charity to take me in tow. I am lonely like yourself, and very impatient to make the time pass till I can return home, and I am sure your company will help to do so. Is it a bargain?"

"My dear fellow, nothing would give me greater pleasure. I am not quite a pauper, Melstrom, and if you will lend me sufficient to get out of Homburg, I shall receive a communication from my bankers in the course of a week. But what will the Countess say?"

"I don't understand you."

"Will she not be shocked if she hears that you have taken up with a man of my Bohemian proclivities — with a gambler, for I tell you plainly that I find my greatest excitement at the tables or in the cards—with a disbeliever in love, marriage, women, virtue — all the good old fables, in fact, which have been instilled into our minds with our mother's milk, and which so few of us credit afterwards?"

Anthony Melstrom looked serious.

"Strange to say," he answered, "though I have known you so short a time, I do not believe you to be half so bad as you would make yourself out to be. But were it so, I am afraid my mother does not take enough interest in my career to be either shocked or pleased by the company I keep. In fact, she has never asked what it might be, so I consider myself at liberty to choose it for myself. And when the month of probation is over, I shall try and induce you to accompany me back to Gardenholme."

Oliver Fosbrooke started.

"To Gardenholme?" he ejaculated. "Oh no! I could not go with you to Gardenholme."

"Why not? You say you know the place,

and must remember how charming the old abbey and the surrounding gardens are."

Fosbrooke passed his handkerchief across his brow.

"Yes. I can remember perfectly. Is it much changed from—from five-and-twenty years ago?"

"I believe not. My mother always prides herself on keeping it up as it was in the old days. Did you know my grandfather, Fosbrooke?"

"No. He had been dead for some years before I became acquainted with your father."

"But you must have known my father's sister, Lady Diana Melstrom, who lived with him till she died. Poor Aunt Diana! I never saw her, of course, but I have heard she was lovely. Our old butler says she was the toast of the county."

"What did she die of?" demanded Fosbrooke, as he stooped to recover his serviette.

"I am not quite sure. I believe it was from a fall from her horse, or some dreadful accident, but my mother never cared to speak of it. Indeed, I hardly think she knows herself. And Aunt Diana was such a favourite sister of my father's that he could never bear to mention her name. Although she was such a beauty, we have not a single likeness of her. He smashed them all after her death, and destroyed every memento of her. It seems a great pity!"

"Does — does this Miss Paget you spoke of remember your poor aunt?" asked Fosbrooke.

"Oh no! How should she? She only came to live with us a few years before my father's death — when I was about five, I think. She never knew any of the family before that."

"Well, I am not sure whether I should like to see Gardenholme again or not, Melstrom. It would contain many sweet and bitter memories for me, for I esteemed your father highly. But for your sake I am sure I should like to be introduced to Miss Lily Osprey."

"You shall be introduced to her when she

is my wife, if not before," replied the lad, proudly.

"Don't shout till you're out of the wood, Anthony. A year is a long time to a girl of nineteen. You may find a rival in the field."

"Never! She is as true as steel."

"Others have said that before you. But come, my friend, the supper is finished, and it is early morning. We had better go to bed. To-morrow, since you wish it, we will journey on together, and I will try what I can do to make your exile pleasanter to you. Good night! I suppose I ought to thank you again for what you have done for me, or saved me from, and I do thank you for the generous impulse that prompted the deed. That, and a certain look in your eyes that brings back the remembrance of happier days to me, have made me your friend for life, Anthony. I am not a good man—I do not profess to be—but you need never fear for me. I will cut off my right hand before I abuse the trust and confidence you have shown in me to-night."

CHAPTER III.

IN THE COUNTESS'S BOUDOIR.

EW people with unbiassed minds would have been found ready to endorse Anthony Melstrom's generous estimate of his elder brother's character, for to the majority Lord Culwarren was an effete, weak-minded, and intensely conceited young man. Having no occasion to work for his living, and being strongly desirous to court popularity, he tried to pose as a genius, and spent his time in writing bad novels and worse poetry, which no one read but tuft-hunters, and for the appearance of which he largely indemnified his publishers. Still, he and his mother continued to believe that his non-success was caused solely by the envy and malice of less favoured writers, and that the day must dawn when his brilliant talents, combined with his high station, would make the world fall down and worship him. They formed of themselves a little mutual admiration society, of which each member was always ready to put the other in a good temper, despite of all discouragements from without. So the young Earl wrote, and Lady Culwarren admired, and chose to believe that every one viewed them in the same light they did themselves.

About a month after the occurrence related in the last chapter, the Countess was seated in her boudoir awaiting the arrival of her son. She kept a suite of apartments for her own use in the left wing of the house, which was shut off by baize doors from the rest of the establishment. Here, in a gorgeously furnished apartment, the walls, and tables, and étagères of which were covered with paintings, marble statuettes, rare china, and ivory carvings, it was her ladyship's pleasure to take her breakfast and receive such of her intimates as desired an audience of her, before she appeared en grande toilette at the luncheon-table. Culwarren was naturally the most frequent and the most favoured guest who ever knocked at the boudoir door. Indeed, he usually spent all his mornings there, composing his literary rubbish under the supervision of his mother, who was about as competent to advise as he was to write. But a sincere, though selfish affection existed between the Countess and her son, and the readiness with which she called out "Entrez" in answer to his summons, showed the satisfaction she felt at his arrival. It would fain have astonished any one who had been told that the Earl of Culwarren resembled his once beautiful mother, to have seen them together for the first time. He was a tall, slender young man, with brown eyes, and dark, crisp hair, which he wore rather long, in imitation of Tennyson and Swinburne, whilst she had a head of bright golden locks. But she had become in-oculated with the prevailing fashion of dyeing her hair and painting her face, which, as she was now in her fifty-second year, made her age only more apparent. But she had been a toasted beauty, and she could not forget it, and so she attempted to hide the ravages of Time by Art, and fondly hoped that no one but her maid was in the secret. Attired in a peach-coloured robe de chambre, trimmed with costly lace, and with a fanciful cap upon her head, Lady Culwarren looked like a large and handsome doll, freshly turned out of the maker's hands, before any of its curls had been ruffled, or the rosy hue of its lips kissed away. She saluted her son, though, very affectionately, and discovered at the first glance that something had disturbed him.

"Why, my dear Culwarren, what is the matter?" she exclaimed, as she held his hand. "Nothing unpleasant appeared in the papers about 'An Aristocratic Secret,' I hope? Because, if so, you must certainly not let Toad-eater have your next novel. I gave him carte blanche to buy up the critics, in order that you should have favourable reviews."

"No, mother, it's not that. There hasn't been time for the book to be reviewed yet."

"Nonsense, dear boy! It has been out more than a week, and naturally the critics would read a novel from your pen sooner than they would those of the dozens of common authors who make a living by literature."

"Perhaps so. Still, I have seen nothing of it."

"What makes you look so gloomy, then? You have had something on your mind for weeks past. Come! what is the use of beating about the bush in this way? Tell me all about it. I may be able to help you."

The young Earl threw himself into a chair and leaned his head thoughtfully upon his hand.

"You have remarked it then, mother?" he said, with a melodramatic air.

"How could I fail to remark it, Culwarren? Whom do I ever trouble my head about, except it is yourself? You know that you are my chief care—that you occupy my undivided heart, and always have done so—with the exception,

of course, of that affection which was due to
your late lamented father."

"You have forgotten my brother Melstrom,"
said the Earl. At the mention of that name
the alteration in Lady Culwarren's voice and
manner was painfully apparent. From having
been earnest and affectionate it became hard
and cold, as though the very subject were
distasteful to her. She could not forgive the
younger son, perhaps, for being so much handsomer, brighter, and a greater favourite with
the world than his elder brother.

"Anthony!" she ejaculated, indifferently.
"Oh, yes! he is well enough, poor fellow, and
his father made an absurd fuss over him. But
you are my own child, Culwarren—a Fairley
no less in feature than in mind. You take after
my family, and you have always held the first
place in my affections."

"And you are very fond of Lily also, mother,
are you not? I fancy you would find it almost
as hard to part with her as with myself."

"Well, naturally, Culwarren. You have often

heard me speak of the strong attachment that existed between my dead sister and myself, and her child has been like a real daughter to me. But why look so conscious? Have you really come this morning to make a confession to me?"

"What sort of a confession?" asked the Earl, with a conceited smile.

"One that I have been expecting to hear for a long time—that you have come to the conclusion that since Lily has spent so much of her life with us, it would be a pity for her ever to seek another home."

"Don't laugh at me, mother, for I'm very much in earnest. I'm over head and ears in love with her, and I want to marry her. There! now the murder's out."

"Well?"

"*Well!* You are not surprised, nor vexed, nor startled by my announcement? For this is no light fancy on my part, mother, to be taken up to-day and put down to-morrow. I want to make Lilian Osprey the Countess of Culwarren.

You are sure you will like to see her sitting in your seat?"

Lady Culwarren rose with dignity, and crossing the room, imprinted a kiss upon the forehead of her son. It was not an ardent kiss—as mothers' kisses go—but then she had just been made up, and had her paint and powder to think of. But the embrace was worth more than it appeared, only there are circumstances under which one cannot afford to be too affectionate.

"My darling boy, it is just what I have been secretly longing for. Lily is a sweet, affectionate, docile girl, who will make you a charming wife and me an excellent daughter. I congratulate you both with all my heart."

"Yes! But what about Anthony?"

"What about Anthony? I do not understand you, Culwarren."

"Why, you know there were love passages between him and Lily before he left home—that they even considered themselves engaged to each other."

" Nonsense ! nonsense ! " exclaimed the Countess, "there was nothing of the sort. I utterly forbade them to think of such a thing. Anthony may have disobeyed me — he has always been of an intractable and rebellious nature — but I have implicit faith in my niece, and I can vouch for her never having written to him, or hardly spoken of him, since their separation."

"Still, she may not have forgotten him, mother, and somehow I don't think she has. If I formally offer her my hand, she may not see fit to accept it."

Lady Culwarren laughed incredulously.

"With your coronet in it! What an absurd idea! Really, Culwarren, you are ridiculously modest. Do you mean to tell me that if you, with your title, and your wealth, and your genius and good looks, were to ask Lily Osprey to be your wife, she would refuse you? You must think very little of yourself, or very little of her, to entertain such an idea. You put me out of all patience by even supposing it."

But the Earl shook his head, and was silent.

"Why, Culwarren, what in the name of wonder do you expect? You cannot really suppose that Lily is secretly fretting after that scapegrace brother of yours? He must have had twenty other love affairs by this time."

"Perhaps, mother. I may be altogether wrong, but I don't think she favours *my* suit. To tell you the truth, I have approached the subject with her several times lately, and she has always repulsed me. This morning we met in the corridor, and she looked so lovely in her simple muslin dress, I felt as if I could not restrain my feelings any longer; but directly she found out to what my words were leading, she ran away and joined Miss Paget, and has refused to leave her side since."

"All modesty, my dear son, and maidenly bashfulness. You young fellows who knock about the world and come in contact with so many women unworthy of the name, cannot understand the feelings of alarm that assail an innocent girl when first she is made love to.

Perhaps, also, Lily is uncertain of my approbation, and dutiful enough to wish to ascertain it before giving you encouragement."

"Do you really think so, mother?"

"I really do. As for that other business, you need not waste a thought upon it. It never amounted to anything, and has been forgotten long ago. Besides, such a marriage would be impossible. Lily is entirely under my control, and neither of them has sufficient money to maintain a suitable position. I would never give my consent to it. Anthony will have nothing until my death, except a paltry three hundred a year which he inherits on coming of age."

"Why, mother, he is twenty-one to-day, is he not? By George! I had quite forgotten it!"

"So had I, my dear; but the birthdays of younger sons are of no consequence. By the way, though, it reminds me that I saw a letter in his handwriting amongst that pile. Read it to me, Culwarren. I dare say, as usual, it will contain nothing to amuse or interest us; but as it has come, it may as well be opened."

She lay back in her chair and commenced to sip her cup of chocolate, as the Earl rose and selected his brother's letter from the rest. But as he glanced at its contents, he grew pale with excitement.

"Mother," he exclaimed, "he has returned to England. Anthony wrote this letter from London last night, to request a carriage may be sent for him and his friend, Mr. Fosbrooke, to the 'Culwarren Arms' at Dearham to-day. He says he is determined to spend his twenty-first birthday at home. I guess the reason of this unexpected return. I know why he is coming back the very moment he is his own master, and no longer under your control. He means to take Lily from me. He will assert the rights of their previous engagement to ask her to become his wife, and from the moment he re-enters the Abbey, *my* chances are gone for ever." And Culwarren began to pace up and down the room like a caged panther. But the Countess would not allow there was any cause for her son's alarm.

"You are talking like a child, Culwarren," she said, somewhat impatiently, "and will spoil everything if you are not careful. I have already told you to leave this matter to me. Say nothing of Anthony's expected return downstairs. It will be quite time enough to announce the news when I appear at the luncheon-table."

"But Anthony desires the carriage shall go for them at twelve."

"I can't help that. He should have shown a little more consideration than to take us so completely unawares. I shall tell him it was not convenient. And who is this friend, Mr. Fosbrooke, of whom his last letters have been so full? Why should he foist him off on Gardenholme as well as himself? He knows how I hate strangers. But Anthony was always selfish and inconsiderate from a child. I pity the woman who marries him. The carriage will not start for them till three, however—I am not going to have my servants disturbed at their dinner—and by that time, Culwarren, Lily Osprey shall be your affianced wife."

" Mother ! is it possible ? "

" It is more than possible—it is certain. As soon as you have left me, I shall send for Lily and speak to her myself. She cannot refuse me. I have brought her up from an infant, and been both father and mother to her. She is more daring than I take her for if she presumes to question my right to settle her choice of a husband. If she has foolishly cherished any idea of allegiance to your brother, she shall at once dismiss it."

" But supposing she finds that impossible ? Supposing her heart is so seriously involved that she refuses to give Anthony up? The idea that any other man may possess her drives me mad. If that should come to pass, I believe——"

" It *never* shall come to pass, Culwarren. Trust me to prevent it. And now go, in order that I may send my maid to find Lily at once. Depend that all shall be right when we meet again."

The Earl kissed his mother's blooming cheek with filial discretion, and left her to carry out his matrimonial designs.

CHAPTER IV.

"DRAWN INTO THE NET."

WHEN Lady Culwarren's maid went in search of Miss Osprey, she found her in the music-room, with her head upon Miss Paget's shoulder, listening with languid, closed eyes to the glorious melodies of Mozart. The music-room at Gardenholme was an institution. Both the Earl and his mother sang well, and Miss Paget was an excellent musician. Lady Culwarren, therefore, had had every inducement since her husband's death to keep up the apartment in the style in which he had loved to see it. It was a saloon, or wide corridor, connecting the rooms on the lower floor, and was closed at either end by folding doors. The floor was composed of tesselated wood, the walls of oak panelling, and the dome-shaped ceiling was painted with a representation of the apotheosis of Saint Cecilia, the patroness of melody. In the centre of the room, opposite the high, carved-wood mantelpiece, there was a chamber organ, the use of which was known only to Miss Paget. On a raised platform at one end stood a grand pianoforte and a harp in its leathern cover, and at the other a bookcase containing a complete library of music by ancient and modern composers. About the room were cases of violins, guitars, flutes, and concertinas—of every instrument, in fact, which Lord Culwarren had thought fit to take up for a few months, or weeks, or days, as the fancy seized upon or deserted him. Lately, however, he had come to the conclusion that a mandoline was the fittest medium for a poet's fantasies, and so the others had been left in peace. A few couches ranged round the walls, and a table with writing materials for copying or composing music, completed the furniture of the room, which was the favourite retreat of Miss Paget and Lily Osprey, who was

ardently attached to her. As they sat together
at the organ now, they formed a charming
contrast. Lily was really lovely. The brothers'
contest for her possession became no marvel
when one saw her perfectly formed figure,
rounded as that of a child, and yet supple as
an Eastern houri's — her long, almond-shaped
eyes dark as night, her blue-black hair without
any gloss upon it, her delicate complexion, and
curved lips tinged like the rose-leaf. She was,
in fact, too pretty to be very strong-minded
or reliable, and under her aunt's arbitrary
control was as plastic as warm wax in the
hands of a moulder. Miss Paget, on the contrary,
was a woman of great character and determination. Her pale features, chiselled like
those of a statue, must have been very handsome in her younger days, and her hair was
soft and abundant; but she always hid it away
beneath a mob-cap, and dressed in grave colours,
and a style that made her look much older
than she was. But she was a thorough gentle-
woman and one of great accomplishments, and

it was evident from the free and unembarrassed manner in which caresses passed between her and the ladies of the establishment that she was not looked on as an ordinary companion at Gardenholme. Indeed, she was more like a dear friend to Lady Culwarren than a dependent, being a distant connection of the late Earl, and having been especially recommended by him to the care and consideration of his Countess. As Lily Osprey heard the message sent to her by Lady Culwarren, she jumped up from her caressing position, almost with a look of alarm.

"Oh, Miss Paget, what can Aunt Emily want with me?"

"How can *I* tell, Lily? A book fetched, perhaps, or a note written. Don't keep her waiting."

"But I went in and kissed her the first thing this morning. I wonder if Culwarren is with her?"

"What difference can that make to you? Your aunt would not have sent for you if she did not require you. Really, Lily, I think you are growing lazier every day."

"I hate to be called away in the midst of your music," said the girl, still lingering.

"Then go and do her ladyship's bidding without further delay, and you will be the sooner able to return to it. I will wait for you here."

Miss Osprey left the room, but very slowly. Her instincts warned her of what was coming, and she felt as nervous of the approaching interview as the little bird does that flutters nearer and nearer to the serpent's sinuous body and glittering, cruel eyes. There was something not unlike the subtlety of the serpent, too, in the fawning way in which Lady Culwarren received the poor little bird. For she had a strong suspicion that Lily *did* retain some romantic memory of her younger cousin, and her intention was to surround the girl, as it were, with so vivid a picture of all she owed to her love and protection, as to leave her no means of escape when asked to make some return for all she had received. So the Countess embraced her niece on meeting with more tha her usual tenderness, and drew her down to sit beside her on a little couch by the window.

"My dearest girl," she commenced, "I have scarcely seen you this morning, and you cannot think how I miss the sight of your sweet face. It is very selfish of me, perhaps; but I am jealous of your company being so much monopolised by strangers."

"I have been sitting with Miss Paget, Aunt Emily, in the music-room."

"It is all the same thing, my child. You were not *here*. And you know how much I love you, Lily."

"I know how good you have always been to me."

"That is a very cold way of expressing it, my dear. Others have been good to you, I dare say—Miss Paget, for example—but I have cared for you for my beloved sister's sake, and loved you only second to your cousin Culwarren. Have you ever felt the want of a mother, Lily?"

"Never, dear Aunt Emily," cried the girl, warmly. "I have often said how much luckier

I am than other girls, for I have had two mothers—yourself and Miss Paget—to bring me up between you, and from the affection you have lavished on me, I have never had an opportunity to regret my own. Indeed—*indeed*, I am not ungrateful."

"I am sure you are not, my love. It is quite true, Lily, that but for me you would never have had a home. Your poor parents were sadly imprudent, and left you, poor little orphan, with scarcely a halfpenny in the world. You will have a very small annual allowance, love, on attaining your majority, but it is a trifle compared to what I have spent on your education alone. But I took you to my bosom gladly and thankfully for my dear sister's sake, and if I have ever failed in my duty to you, tell me of the error, and it shall be rectified."

"Oh! dear Aunt Emily, how *can* you speak so to me, who owe everything I possess to your goodness and bounty?"

"I ask nothing in return, my darling, except to see you and my dear Culwarren happy.

We have been talking so much of you this morning."

"Of *me*, Aunt Emily?"

The child's cheek paled at once. She knew her instincts had not led her wrong.

"Yes, of you. Why not? Do we not both love you dearly? Who, indeed, have we to care for or to love, if not yourself, my Lily?"

"Dear Aunt Emily, I can say no more than I have done already. I owe my home and all I possess to you, and I would lay down my life to prove my gratitude."

The Countess laughed immoderately at Lily's enthusiasm, and patted her delicately tinted cheek.

"Oh! we don't ask quite such a sacrifice from you as that, my love. But you are happy with us, are you not?"

Lily hesitated a moment before she replied: "Yes, aunt, I am happy."

"You love Gardenholme, I am sure, and your many pleasures here. You would be sorry to lose the society of dear Miss Paget or the affection of Culwarren and myself?"

"Very, very sorry. Have I not already told you that I am happy?"

"I am rejoiced to hear it. I wish both my beloved children could say the same thing. But Culwarren is *not* happy, Lily."

"Culwarren not happy? Why?" demanded the girl, trembling for the answer she felt she should receive.

"Can you ask me that question, dear? You are a woman, and must have a woman's instincts. Are your eyes not opened? Is it possible you are still blind to the great love my boy bears for you?"

"Oh, aunt, pray don't say so! Pray don't go on," cried her niece, with clasped hands and a look of the utmost distress. Lady Culwarren saw that it was no mock modesty that dictated this appeal to her, but she continued without mercy, though with a considerable access of dignity.

"Why should I not say so? You do not mean to tell me, Lily, that you would dare to trifle with his happiness and mine; that after all the years of tender solicitude I have spent upon you, you would break away from us like a stranger. Is it too much in return to ask you to listen to what I have to say?"

"Go on, dear aunt," replied the girl, in a stifled voice.

"Culwarren loves you," continued the Countess, in a stiffer and prouder tone, "and he wishes to make you his wife. There is hardly a family in England from which he might not choose a Countess as fancy dictated to him; but he prefers to confer that honour upon you, and I, too, am anxious to call you in reality what you have so long been from adoption—my daughter. I can hardly believe, then, that you intend to fly in my face and disappoint all our hopes by a rude rejection of his offer."

"Oh, no!" said Lily, who was shaking like an aspen-leaf, "I would not be ungrateful to you or him for all the world; but, still, if I cannot—that is to say, it would be so unfair——"

"What would be unfair?" demanded the Countess, with chilling precision. "Do you mean to say you do not love your cousin?"

" Of course I love him, but not in that way."

" Not in *what* way ? "

Lily blushed violently, but remained silent.

" What can you know of the different ways of love ? Who has presumed to speak to you on such a subject ? "

" No one, Aunt Emily. Only I thought——"

" You must not think ; your duty is to obey. Come, Lily, tell me that you will make my dear Culwarren happy, and you will never hear another reproachful word from me."

" But *can* I make him happy ? " asked Lily, sadly.

" Of course you can, and me also. I have planned a marriage between you for years past, and am delighted my beloved son sees it in the same light as I do. But you are still silent. You really intend, then, to give me trouble in this matter ? "

" No, no ! I will do anything you wish. You have a right to command my actions."

" Then I may tell Culwarren that it is a settled thing ? "

" How can I say 'No' in the face of all of which you have reminded me ?" replied the girl, with the tears upon her face.

Lady Culwarren kissed them off.

" There, there! I will ask no more at present. Dry your eyes, dear child, and let me salute the future Countess of Culwarren. You have said quite enough, my darling, and I feel sure you will never go back from your word. Come, Lily, don't be a little goose. The prospect of marriage is always startling at first to an unsophisticated girl, but you will learn to look back on this day as the happiest of your life."

The girl rose from her seat and sobbed for a few minutes in Lady Culwarren's arms, then, drying her eyes, she gave her one or two hasty kisses and quickly left the apartment. Her first impulse was to seek Miss Paget and tell her of the terrible misfortune which had befallen her. It is true that, notwithstanding the affection that existed between them, the reserved and staid demeanour of Lady Culwarren's companion, as well as the superiority of her age, had prevented, hitherto, any very warm confidences passing between her and Miss Osprey ; but all that Lily remembered at this moment was that Miss Paget was the only person to whom she could tell her perplexity, and that if she did not tell it to some one her heart would break. She did not expect to hear Miss Paget blame the action of her employer nor the presumption of the Earl. That would have been in direct opposition to the perfect respect with which she acquiesced in every decision arrived at by the house of Culwarren. But she did think that she would have bidden her be true to the higher nature she had sedulously striven to cultivate in her, and to bravely resist all counsel in such a case but that of her own heart. She found the companion still seated at the organ, and walking straight up to her, she laid her head down on her bosom and burst into a flood of tears.

"What on earth is the matter, Lily?" exclaimed Miss Paget, as she removed her hands from the keys, and regarded her young friend with surprise. "What has occasioned this distress? Has some clumsy servant trodden on your precious

Bijou again, or does the moulting canary still refuse his food ?"

It was a peculiarity of Miss Paget that though apparently formed by nature to be all that was soft, and womanly, and refined, she invariably professed to believe that the most violent emotion might spring from the meanest causes. She ridiculed, in fact, all feeling, affirmed there were no misfortunes in this world worthy the tears of a reasonable being, and that we had but to bring a powerful will to bear upon our determination *not* to suffer to make all circumstances alike indifferent to us. She had little sympathy, then, as may be supposed, for weakness of any sort, and evinced the profoundest contempt for those hapless mortals who permit themselves to be crushed by the troubles which accompany all earthly careers.

"Don't laugh at me, Miss Paget," sobbed Lily. "It is nothing. I shall be myself again presently."

"If it be nothing, I sincerely hope you will. Right or wrong, people generally fancy they have something to weep and wail for. Few will confess to doing it for pleasure."

"Of course there is a reason. You might guess that, Miss Paget."

"I can guess more! I guess the reason itself. Your aunt has caused these tears by urging you to take a step that appears distasteful to you."

Lily looked up in astonishment.

"How could you know before I told you?"

"By studying your character, Lily. Do you think we have lived so short a time together that I have had no opportunity of reading your mind, and thoughts, and wishes? Why, for twelve long years we have dwelt under the same roof."

"I know it, Miss Paget, and I have heard that my late uncle, for the sake of some dead memories, regarded you as a no less sacred charge to him than myself."

At the mention of Lord Culwarren's goodness to her, the corners of the companion's mouth worked visibly, but she exercised the strong will she was so fond of recommending to others upon the muscles of her face, and after a moment's struggle it had settled down into its usual placid, though rather weary expression.

"You are right, Lily. He was a true friend to me. May God bless him for it! And in return I have tried to do my duty to those he left behind him. I am not very demonstrative in my affection, but you must have seen I care for you."

"Indeed, I hope so. Your kindness to me, Miss Paget, and to—to—my cousin Anthony——"

"Your cousin Anthony? Why do you particularise him? Why not include Culwarren? I have watched you all grow up together from children. What preference have I shown between the three?"

At this question Lily became confused.

"Oh, I don't know. Only I thought — I have always fancied you liked Anthony best."

"Your fancy is the reflection of your own mind, my dear; though I confess I have always taken a strong interest in Anthony's character—partly, perhaps, because nobody else seemed to do so. It is wild and fitful enough to make an anxious study for any one who is concerned in his future career—far too wild and fitful for a husband. Lily, Culwarren will bring far more peace into your domestic life."

"Oh, Miss Paget! do you, then, know——"

"That her ladyship sent for you this morning to make you an offer of Culwarren's hand, and that you shrink from accepting it because of some foolish fancy in the past. Yes, Lily, I have guessed so far. I have seen in what direction the hopes of Lady Culwarren and her son were tending for the last twelve months, and felt sure of the issue to which they must arrive."

"And what do you advise me to do?" cried the girl, with trembling eagerness.

"Never to look further than to-day," replied Miss Paget, vehemently; "never to remember that yesterday has been, or to-morrow must inevitably be. That is a folly into which your heart may tempt you; but if you wish to battle successfully with the world, Lily, you must ignore the very existence of a heart."

She pushed the girl's clinging arms away from her as she spoke, and rose to her full height. Her face was blanched with the force of her feeling, though her lips were pressed tightly together to prevent the expression of it.

"Oh, Miss Paget," cried Lily, "you frighten me! I have never heard you speak like this before."

But the companion did not seem to hear that she was spoken to. She had passed away from the scene in which she stood, to a world peopled by her own fancy, or remembrance.

"I repeat it," she exclaimed, as she paced up and down the room. "You are a woman, and your heart can never lead you to any happiness. On the contrary, it may plunge you into irretrievable error—may even persuade you to place your faith in such a *lie* as Love——"

"Miss Paget—Miss Paget!"

"To believe that it exists," continued the companion, vehemently; "that the fables we hear of its delights, its purity, its trust, are not huge frauds invented to tempt weak fools to their destruction — to believe that man is not the natural enemy of woman, and the *thing* which he calls Love, the commonest weapon with which he strikes her to the ground."

Lily burst into a fresh flood of tears. Miss Paget seemed to wake as from a dream. In a moment she was herself again.

"Forgive me, Lily. I am afraid I have forgotten my part of monitor. What was it you asked of me? My counsel; it is this. Do as your aunt wishes—marry Culwarren. Please the world; take all the satisfaction that rank and wealth can offer you, and be happy."

"How *can* I be happy upon such terms as these? There is no happiness left in the world for me. Oh, Anthony!——"

"Anthony! It is as I suspected, then, Lily; and that old folly is standing in the light of your future prospects."

"Oh, have I no pride, no self-respect," exclaimed the girl, as she dashed away her tears, "that I should let my heart be read like an open book? He must have forgotten me. Our love was but a childish folly—the natural affection of a boy and girl brought up together. It is best forgotten—blotted from my memory. And yet——"

"And yet you want to hug this false sentiment

to your bosom, instead of thankfully casting it away to make room for the real life that is opening before you. Lily, I am ashamed of you. Think of all you owe your aunt and cousin — of the happiness you will bestow on them. And think of me, too, dear child. I take the greatest interest in your welfare, and would not have you cast out upon the world to meet temptations which might prove too strong for you. Once married to Culwarren, I shall feel that you are safe."

She advanced to where the girl stood, and folding her arms around her, pressed her cold lips to her forehead.

"There are so many dangers in this world," she repeated, murmuringly; "so many which you have never dreamt of; and I would have you safely sheltered, my darling, from them all. Say that you will marry Lord Culwarren, Lily, and forget the other."

"I will marry Culwarren," replied the girl, in a faltering voice. "It seems my duty to do so; but I shall never, *never* forget, Miss Paget, till I am dead and buried."

"God help you!" murmured the companion.

CHAPTER V.

THE ABBEY GARDEN.

HAD the proprietors of Gardenholme been stirring at four o'clock on that particular August morning, they would have found a trespasser on their premises in the person of Oliver Fosbrooke, who had arrived at the "Culwarren Arms" the night before, and slipped out of the house without giving young Melstrom any notice of his intentions. But the shutters of the Abbey were still closed, and not a soul was to be seen anywhere, for Lady Culwarren's servants brought their London habits into the country with them, and saw no necessity for rising early in the service of a mistress who never made her own appearance before noon. So that when Mr. Fosbrooke came walking quietly along the edge of the grass, looking around him apparently with the greatest interest, no gardener nor servant of any sort attempted to bar his progress or to ask his business at that hour of the morning in Lord Culwarren's grounds. Not but what he looked a gentleman from head to foot, and far brighter and, perhaps, a shade less reckless than when Anthony Melstrom first met him in the " Hôtel des Papilons"—still, he was attired with a carelessness seldom seen amongst his class in this country, and servants are apt to judge a man by his clothes. He wore a velveteen shooting coat of a peculiar shade of golden brown ; round his throat was knotted a silk handkerchief of the brightest crimson, and the legs of his trousers, which he had turned up with an evident view to avoiding contact with the dew-laden grass, displayed a pair of fawn-coloured boots, with pearl buttons, which were very un-English in their style and manufacture. As he trod the paths of the Abbey grounds, his blue eyes looked very sad and thoughtful. He seemed to recognise each stick and stone of the place, but he stepped carefully, as though anxious to be neither seen nor heard by the inhabitants. The scene which surrounded him was a lovely one, for the sun never shone upon a fairer English residence than Gardenholme, which was situated in the very heart of smiling Surrey. The grounds were extensive, and a large portion of them were left, at Lord Culwarren's request, to flourish according to the laws of Nature. He had heard of the late Lord Lytton's garden at Kneb-worth, and hoped, perhaps, by imitating his favourite haunts, to become inspired by some of that great author's poetic fancies, or to catch the art of writing in the most elegant English that has ever been transcribed for the benefit of novel-readers. Certainly, though it might be difficult to compete with that romantic retreat which, it was said, irresistibly reminded the spectator of the famous garden of the Emperor Hadrian at Tivoli, where he endeavoured to perpetuate his recollections of classic Greece, Gardenholme was as beautiful a specimen of a pleasure ground —assisted by art to look more natural than nature—as could possibly be found. The little

lake that intersected it, winding sinuously between the verdant swards which lay immediately
beneath the terrace, was fringed with unpruned
bushes that dipped their feathery boughs into
the water—whilst from the grass reared a myriad
of blossom beads—of golden cowslips, and delicate
harebells, and fragrant woodruffe, which no spades
nor scythes were ever permitted to uproot or mow
down.

Here Lord Culwarren was used to pace when
in the agonies of composition, trying to make
his eye in a fine frenzy roll, whilst he knit his
brows, and thrust his fingers through his hair,
and trampled the innocent flowerets underfoot
for nothing. But Oliver Fosbrooke knew naught
of the present Earl or his poetic ravings—all his
thoughts were occupied with the past, before
the genius of the family had been dreamt of.

"Here is the very spot where I first saw
her," he said, inwardly, as he halted for a
moment before the old Norman porch.

"How well I remember it! The meet of
the hounds was held here in her brother's reign,

and she was allowed to join it for the first time. By Jove! what a beautiful creature she was! I can see her graceful figure now as she sprang into the saddle, and the golden curls she flung back so carelessly over her dark blue riding-habit. I know I lost my heart to her then and there—fool that I was!—and I suppose that is the reason I have never felt it beating since. If I were as susceptible now as I was then, I should surely feel a little sentimental over the memories of three-and-twenty years ago. But I can't. Perhaps I've suffered too much. Perhaps I've sinned too much. Perhaps I've tried to drown recollection when it became a misery to me, until I've stamped out all the softness of my nature. But anyway, it's the truth. The remembrance of her beauty and my passion has lost its power over me. I can even contemplate her grave without a sigh. And yet there is something terrible in thinking of all that loveliness mouldering in corruption. Poor Diana! It was a mistake from beginning to end. The less said about it the better."

Fosbrooke left the porch suddenly as the last thought passed through his mind, and did not once glance backwards as he strode round the corner. But here the sight of a small oriel window, shaded by a dark red blind, seemed to make him flinch as though something had struck him in the face.

He stopped short, drew his hand quickly across his eyes, as though to convince himself he was awake, and then stared at the casement in mute astonishment.

"Surely this room lay at the other side of the Abbey?" he said, confusedly. "How can I have made such an error? I never intended to have come here. I—I—would rather have not seen it again."

He took out a silk handkerchief and drew it once or twice lightly across his brow.

"Have I been a fool," he asked himself, "to come back to Gardenholme at all? It seemed so easy to forget when far away. But every inanimate object stirs a fresh remembrance in me. My dear injured friend, my almost brother,

Culwarren, and *she*, too, poor girl! I wonder
if their spirits are about me now? Well, well!
I have yielded to an impulse I could not resist,
and it is too late to draw back again. But it
is as well I have prepared myself for the effect
the old place might have on me. I shall be
my own master now, whatever happens, and
du reste, if memories are still vivid, they shall
not prove too strong for me. Hitherto I have
stamped them *down*, henceforward I will stamp
them *out*."

Here a slight movement of the red blind,
caused probably by the morning breeze finding
its way into the half-opened casement, made
Fosbrooke start. He feared it might be followed
by the appearance of some one whom his footsteps had aroused from sleep.

"It will not do for me to be caught skulk-
ing about Gardenholme as though I had some
evil design upon the plate-chest. I am known to
no one here, and might have some difficulty in
accounting for my presence. I had better find
my way back to Dearham as quickly as I can.

I don't want even Anthony to guess where my
morning stroll has led me."

He did not loiter another moment, but
walked rapidly through the wet grass, scaring
the blackbirds and thrushes at their morning
meal, until he had gained the outskirts of the
grounds that immediately surrounded the Abbey.

" How lovely it all is!" thought Fosbrooke,
as he turned to survey the scene he had passed
through; "the place is hardly changed since I
last saw it. Foliage a little thicker in the
shrubberies, perhaps, and the gardens not kept
up quite so carefully as they were in my friend's
time. But if all I hear of Lord Culwarren be
true, he is no more fit to manage an estate than
his silly mother. My young friend Anthony,
who appears to be a swan's egg in a duck's
nest, would have made the more creditable earl
of the two. He has the old blood in him—I
can read it in each sparkle of his eye, each
generous impulse of his warm heart and
thoughtless brain. He reminds me, too, at
times, painfully of *her*. He is a son of whom

his father would have been proud—whereas his
brother, from all accounts, appears to be unworthy of the name. That is generally the
way in this world. Well, I will go back to
Anthony and be the first to congratulate the
boy on coming of age."

He turned his steps in the direction of the
shrubbery that skirted the park, until at a
certain point he found the palings low enough
to permit of his vaulting over them into the
high-road. It was evidently not the first time
in his life that Oliver Fosbrooke had left the
grounds of Gardenholme without a blast of
trumpets to herald his departure. Once on the
road to Dearham, which lay about five miles
distant, all Fosbrooke's usual debonair manner
returned to him, and with a cigar in his mouth
and his hands in his pockets, he swung along
at a rapid pace, untroubled, to all outward
appearance, by any deeper thoughts than a desire
for his breakfast, to which a keen appetite en-
gendered by the fresh morning air largely con-
tributed. As he reached the porch of the

"Culwarren Arms," where they had slept the night before, Anthony Melstrom, in a light summer suit of gray, with a rose in his button-hole, and love and expectation glowing in his face, came out to greet him.

"Hullo, Anthony," exclaimed Fosbrooke, as they met each other. "A thousand happy re-turns of the day to you. But what on earth do you mean by being up at this time of the morning? It's not yet seven o'clock. Has the thought of your manhood's honours ·kept you waking?"

"Might I put the same question to *you*, mon cher?" replied Melstrom, with a look of un-mistakable affection, as he clasped the hand of his friend. "These are not the hours that we used to keep at Baden or Homburg — eh, Fosbrooke?"

"Not exactly, my boy; but neither did we go to roost at ten! I think it must have been the unusually primitive hour at which I retired to rest last night that roused me so early. Any-way, I could sleep no longer, so I thought I might as well take the advantage of being in this fine country air to have a stroll."

"*I* have scarcely slept at all," said Anthony, sadly. "The excitement of being so near my home, and yet knowing nothing of what awaits me there—whether any one will care to see me again—if my presence will even be welcome—has kept me awake. Ah! Fosbrooke, it is hard when a man's own mother takes no interest in him."

"Humph! Perhaps so, dear boy. But as you pass through life you will find so many women willing to undertake her duties, that you will cease to think so much about it. Come, now! You mustn't look so gloomy on your twenty-first birthday."

"Don't mention it, Fosbrooke. I assure you it is no matter of congratulation to me."

"What! Not to become your own master?"

"What good will that do me?"

"Does it not leave you free to woo the pretty cousin about whom you have raved to me at intervals during the last month?"

" To woo is not to win, Fosbrooke. I am
perfectly aware that it was on Lily Osprey's
account that my mother despatched me so
summarily from home a year ago, and that she
has thrown so many obstacles in the way of
my returning now. What her precise object is
I cannot tell, but I feel quite sure that she will
never give her consent to my marrying my cousin."

"Nonsense, man! Don't be so chicken-
hearted. Marry without her consent, then.
You've as good a right to the girl as any one
else. But I guess what you suspect! That
Lady Culwarren is reserving her niece to become the future Countess——"

" That is just it, Fosbrooke," exclaimed
Anthony, eagerly; "and what chance do you
suppose that a younger son will have against
the title and estates of Culwarren? And after
a whole year's separation and silence, too!
Lily is but just nineteen, and very yielding in
disposition. My mother could frighten her into
anything—even into disbelieving that I ever
loved her."

"Well, if she has, let her go to Jericho," cried Fosbrooke, wrathfully; "a woman of that stamp isn't worth fretting after. If she can prefer that long-haired Culwarren, with his absurd æsthetics and self-conceit, to you, and just because he can find her a title, the girl isn't worth your consideration. But until I see it for myself, I won't believe she can have such bad taste."

"Ah, Fosbrooke, you always think too well of me. I never had so kind and generous a friend in my life before."

"Don't make too sure of that, my boy. I may prove yet to be the worst you ever had."

"What, *you*! who have been more like a father than anything else to me?"

Oliver Fosbrooke laughed satirically.

"Rather a harum-scarum kind of father, I'm afraid, young man. What about the places and the people I've introduced you to since our first meeting in the 'Papilons,' when you pulled me by one leg out of the grave? But I must say one thing—it is not easy to corrupt you.

Evil seems to run off your mind, like water from a duck's back — more shame to me for having tried to imbue you with it!"

"You never did try. I took to it as naturally as to mother's milk," replied the young man, laughing. "Well, notwithstanding my anxiety and my fears, Fosbrooke, they were happy, merry days, and I shall often look back upon them with regret, and wish they could come over again."

"And what am I to do without you, Anthony?" said his friend, ruefully. "I have not had the courage to think of it yet. I'm afraid it will be a case of revolvers over again when I haven't the benefit of your youth and freshness to keep my pecker up."

Anthony looked grave.

"Surely," he said, "we shall never *quite* part again, Fosbrooke. I don't feel as if I could bear it."

"I don't see any alternative, my boy. I have accompanied you to the outskirts of your home, as it were, trusting to see you warmly welcomed there, and rewarded with the hand of your pretty cousin. But if that comes to pass, there will be no further room for me, and all I shall have to do will be to say good-bye and go."

"No, no," cried Anthony, warmly; "if ever I marry Lily, you must come and live with us. Promise me, Fosbrooke."

"I don't think domestic happiness and caudle are much in my line, Anthony, nor that, should they come to pass, you will need a witness to them. But promise me, in your turn, that if ever you need a friend or wish to take up a wandering life again, you will think of the man you saved, and come back to share my ramblings."

"I will, Fosbrooke, I *will*," replied the lad, in a broken voice.

"And now, how soon do you intend to put your fate to the touch with regard to Miss Osprey?"

"I wrote to my mother from London yesterday to say that I should arrive home to-day, and bring you with me. The Abbey is sure to be full of guests — it always is — so one more can

make no difference; and I asked her to send
the carriage over for us about noon."

"It was a strange conceit of yours sleeping
in this poky little place, Melstrom, instead of
going straight to Gardenholme."

"Do you think so? You don't know my
mother. She is as particular about her children
keeping up the strictest etiquette with her as if
we were strangers. At least, she has always
been so with me."

"I wonder you venture to take me there with
you at all, Anthony. It will be rather like introducing a bear into a lady's drawing-room."

"Oh, it will be all right now that I have
formally asked her permission. Besides, whatever her faults may be, my mother is not inhospitable, and it would be strange if she could not
accord a welcome to one who was my dear father's
friend."

But as the morning wore on, and no message
arrived from Gardenholme, nor signs of a carriage
to fetch them away, Anthony Melstrom became
fidgety and anxious. He sat in a window of

the "Culwarren Arms," that commanded a view of the road, his fair face flushing more and more with annoyance as the time passed away and brought no intelligence. At last he left his seat and approached Fosbrooke, who was calmly smoking whilst he perused a newspaper in the porch.

"Fosbrooke, there *must* be some mistake. I am sure Culwarren would have ridden over as soon as he could after breakfast, if only to bid me welcome. My letter can never have reached them. They forgot to post it, probably, at the hotel. Would you mind my walking over to Gardenholme by myself and sending back the arriage for you?"

"By no means, my dear boy, if the plan approves itself to you. I think myself there must be some error about it—on your birthday, too. And if only to ease your mind and allay some of the anxiety which I can see is consuming you, you had better walk over and learn the truth."

"I don't feel as if I could wait another moment," cried the lad, with beaming eyes; "it is cruel to be so near and yet not able to see her or speak to her. But I expect I shall run half the way, Fosbrooke, and if I don't meet the carriage on the road, I will despatch it when I get there. Good-bye, and come on as soon as ever it arrives."

And with a nod and a laugh he set off to walk to Gardenholme.

CHAPTER VI.

THE FAMILY LAWYER.

IT was a grand sight (in her own estimation) to see the Countess of Culwarren, in all the majesty of lace and satin, paint and powder, sail into her drawing-room at one o'clock in the afternoon. She never made her appearance before that hour, or she might have missed some of her exacted homage. For a queen could not have made a more royal progress in the precincts of her palace than she did, and every courtier in Gardenholme knew what was expected of him. The ladies must cut short their flirtations or lay aside their needlework, the men put down their newspapers or throw away their cigars, and each one be prepared to welcome their hostess downstairs.

There were several guests at the Abbey, as
Anthony had anticipated, and as her ladyship's
advent was heralded by a tall footman in powder,
who threw open the door and stood sentry over
it, a flutter of expectation ran through the
assembly, which changed to a simultaneous buzz
of admiration and delight as the Countess, robed
in a flowing train of dark blue silk, the golden
curls upon her head dexterously draped by a
fichu of point lace, and her wrists and fingers
laden with jewellery, passed over the threshold,
wreathed in smiles.

"Dear Lady Culwarren, how charming you
look! Just as if you had risen from a bed of
roses," lisped an antiquated old maid, who was
privileged by reason of her exalted rank to peck
at the blooming cheek presented to her.

"The Graces must surely have presided at this
toilette," murmured a poet, a contemporaneous
genius and ardent admirer of the Earl, as he
bent over her hand.

"Oh, Lady Culwarren, the Earl has much to
answer for," cried a lady novelist; "I can neither

eat, sleep, nor rest under the excitement of these
fascinating volumes."

"Marvellous writing for so young a man,"
quoth an ignoramus.

"But then Lord Culwarren is *so* accomplished," sighed a pensive young lady, as she
gazed at his photograph.

"He does not compose badly for his age,"
replied the Countess, with a self-satisfied air;
"indeed, Toadeater thinks all the world of him;
but he is young yet, and, doubtless, by-and-by——"

"By-and-by!" reiterated the authoress. "I
cannot permit your ladyship to utter such
treason, when every one agrees that the Earl's
works are already overflowing with genius. If
they are to go on improving, it will be hard
indeed on us poor literary professionals, who
have to make a living by our labour. What
do you say, Miss Osprey?"

"I—I am hardly a judge," replied Lily,
blushing violently. "I have read so few romances
and——"

Lady Culwarren drew her niece closely to her.

"You must not ask Miss Osprey's opinion, Mrs. Hutterley. There are more reasons than one why my little Lily is not a fit person to sit in judgment on her cousin's writings. It would come rather too near home, darling, would it not? Something like reviewing yourself, eh?"

Lily blushed scarlet, and raised an imploring glance to Lady Culwarren's countenance.

"Oh, Aunt Emily, pray don't!"

"Pray don't *what*, my love? Tell our precious little secret to the company? Oh, you need not be afraid of my discretion, though I do not suppose it will be a secret long. Where *is* our dear Culwarren?"

"I do not know!" replied the girl, in a low voice.

"Or you will not tell—which? You have a grown-up daughter, I believe, Mrs. Hutterley. Do you find her half so shy over her love affairs as I do this little monkey? Ah, dear Miss Paget, I have been wanting you all the morning. You are really too much of a recluse, and when

you know that none of us can get on without
you——"

By this time it had become patent to all
the guests at Gardenholme, that either an engagement had been ratified between Lord Culwarren
and his pretty cousin, or that his mother was
very anxious it should come to pass. But the
announcement had been made in such an uncertain manner, that they hardly knew whether
they were expected to offer their congratulations
or not, and were much relieved when Miss Paget
came to the rescue by changing the subject.

"You are very good to say so, Lady Culwarren. You were asking for the Earl just now.
He is strolling in the grounds with Mr. Ashfold,
who arrived about half an hour ago, and desires
to see you on some particular business. They
promised to be back by luncheon-time."

The Countess elevated her eyebrows, as if
she were not pleased at the intelligence.

"Mr. Ashfold? What on earth can he want
to see me for?"

"That I cannot tell your ladyship. He was

announced whilst Miss Osprey was in your boudoir, and all he told me was that he had come considerably out of his way to call at Gardenholme to-day, and could not possibly leave without an interview."

" Tiresome old man! I call him the raven. His advent is invariably the forerunner of unpleasant news. It makes me quite nervous to hear of his arrival. Gardenholme is threatened with an invasion to-day. My graceless son, Anthony Melstrom, and his friend, Mr. Fosbrooke, are also to be with us this evening."

The involuntary start with which her niece received this unexpected news did not escape the Countess, who turned sharply to her, saying :

"Do try and get out of that schoolgirl fashion of jumping at every trivial thing you hear, Lily. It is neither ladylike nor dignified, and, in the position you are about to fill, you will have to accustom yourself to receive the best or the worst news with the calmness becoming your station. Please remember this, and don't annoy me with such silly tricks again."

"Mr. Melstrom is in England, then?" interposed Miss Paget, with the view of distracting general attention from the unfortunate Lily.

"He is, I am sorry to say, for I do not anticipate much pleasure from his return. I received a letter this morning to say that he and his friend Mr. Fosbrooke—though who on earth this Mr. Fosbrooke is, except some travelling companion whom Anthony has accidentally picked up, I cannot say—are at the 'Culwarren Arms' at Dearham, and wish a carriage sent over for them at noon. By the way, I have quite forgotten to give any order about that carriage, and it is now past one. See to it for me, Miss Paget, if you please. Tell them to start at three. I cannot have my servants' arrangements disturbed for the sake of a thoughtless boy and a man of whom I know nothing."

"Is not Mr. Fosbrooke the gentleman with whom Mr. Melstrom has been travelling in Italy for the last month?" asked her companion.

"He may be. I have a bad memory for

trifles. Anyway, Anthony intends to bring him here, which is excessively annoying, as, if there is anything I dislike more than another, it is being taken by surprise. Why couldn't Anthony have given me longer notice? But he was always selfish and inconsiderate from a child."

At this moment Lord Culwarren and Mr. Ashfold entered the room together. Lily seized the opportunity to creep close to Miss Paget's side and take her hand.

"Oh, Miss Paget!" she whispered, with a gasp of fear, "what *shall* I do?"

"*Do!*" replied the companion, with a frown; "behave as the future Countess of Culwarren should behave."

At which stern rebuke the girl shrank within herself again and was silent.

"Good morning, Mr. Ashfold," commenced the Countess, airily. "I am charmed to see you, of course, but I warn you to be very careful what you say to me, for I have had a good deal to worry me to-day, and I'm in a very bad temper."

"Exactly so. I mean, I thought your lady-ship never indulged in anything so unbecoming," replied the lawyer, in an uncertain manner.

Mr. Ashfold was a little, gray-headed Scots-man, shrewd as a weasel, and able to see through the affectations of a fine lady with any one, but kind-hearted with it all, and excessively nervous directly he found himself beyond the precincts of his dusty office in Chancery Lane. It was this nervous feeling that made him blink like an owl in daylight when in society, and call out, "Exactly so!" whenever he wanted time to think what he should say next.

"Exactly," he continued, rubbing his hands together, and making a kind of half bow, half nod to the assembled company. "Hope I see your ladyship well?"

"Much the same as usual, thank you."

"Exactly so! And Miss Osprey and Miss Paget, too, I trust I find them both in their usual health? Have I disturbed your ladyship too early?"

"You always disturb me too early, Mr.

Ashfold, when you come on business. I hate the very word. It always gives me palpitation of the heart."

"You don't say so!" exclaimed Mr. Ashfold. "Palpitation of the heart. How strange! Delicate and sensitive organ, I am told. I'm not sure I have one myself."

"The world affirms that lawyers never have," said Lord Culwarren, affectedly.

"And *the world* is so sure to be right," retorted Miss Paget. She spoke so seldom that her mere speaking was remarkable, but the sarcasm she threw into her words was more remarkable still.

The lawyer turned at the sound and regarded her fixedly, but she met his gaze as steadily as it was given.

"Exactly so," he said, as he looked away again; "a heart is a luxury we cannot afford——"

"And would not know how to use if you had it," replied Culwarren, trying to be witty.

"Then we are better without it, my lord," said his opponent, smartly. "Personal property which you cannot invest is unremunerative, and, so far, useless."

Lady Culwarren did not like the general laugh which was raised by this repartee at the expense of her son.

"You are not the only unexpected visitor we have to-day, Mr. Ashfold," she said to him. "I have just heard that Mr. Melstrom will be here this evening."

"Ah, indeed! On the 15th of August, too. Very odd. Exactly so."

"His twenty-first birthday. I do not suppose that your visit is connected with his coming of age, Mr. Ashfold," continued the Countess, giggling. "Anthony's vast estates and heavy income will hardly require so much attention as is involved in a special visit from London, before they are made over to their rightful owner."

"Well, no, not exactly," returned the lawyer; "nor did I leave town entirely on your account. I was called to this neighbourhood last evening on urgent business connected with Sir Hugh Loftus. Flesh is weak, and his is failing. No manner of doubt about it. Failing fast."

"Miss Paget," whispered Lily, at this juncture, "I have such a dreadful headache. Do you think Aunt Emily will excuse my appearing at luncheon?"

But the companion did not appear to be listening to her. She was intent upon hearing the conversation passing between Lady Culwarren and the lawyer, and all the answer Lily received was a prolonged, "Hush!"

"I suppose I ought to say I am sorry to hear it, Mr. Ashfold," her ladyship replied; "but we know literally nothing of Sir Hugh. The estates lie a dozen miles apart, and he has lived the life of a hermit for years."

Lord Culwarren, not being interested in the health of Sir Hugh Loftus, had found his way round to his cousin Lily's side by this time, and was regarding her with a look of pleading in his eyes that almost brought the tears into her own.

"Has my mother spoken to you yet?" he whispered.

"Yes—that is to say, why should she not

speak to me, Culwarren?" said the girl, doubling like a hunted hare in the hope of evading her pursuers.

"I mean, has she told you of the great desire of my heart, Lily?" he continued, in the same tone.

"Oh, please do not speak of it now; some one will overhear us. Miss Paget, tell Culwarren this is neither the time nor place to discuss such a subject."

But Lily might as well have appealed to the sofa on which she sat for sympathy or protection. Miss Paget was standing still as a statue, but with every sense riveted on the words proceeding from the lawyer's mouth.

"Exactly so. Like a hermit, and for years past. Odd, isn't it, but doubtless he has his reasons. Sir Hugh is a very disappointed man, my lady. A fine property and plenty of money, but no one to inherit it. The elder son drank himself to death, the younger is—nobody knows where."

"Ah, that younger son, Arthur Loftus. Is

that not his name? Now, what is the truth about him, Mr. Ashfold? You ought to know, since you are in everybody's secrets. There are so many romantic stories afloat about him."

"Exactly so, and some of them true. He was a fine fellow many years ago. Sad story —very sad."

"I have heard the late Earl speak of him, but only once, I think, and that before our marriage. I fancy they were very intimate at one time, but from my husband's manner the subject seemed a painful one to him."

"Very likely, my lady. Mr. Arthur Loftus had more enemies than friends in the county, if all that one hears is correct. He began life with a failure, too. He committed the unpardonable sin—made a mésalliance. When a mere boy he was entrapped into marriage with a—with a—with a—*young person,*" said the little lawyer, finishing up rapidly and with a deprecatory look at the company. The Countess laughed, and tapped him on the shoulder with her Spanish fan.

"There, there, Mr. Ashfold, you need not explain. We understand perfectly, and you are shocking the ladies."

"Exactly so. But after that he fell into various scrapes, and then—he disappeared. A thousand pities. A fine property. Sir Hugh sinking—elder brother dead—and yet he has disappeared. Exactly so."

At that moment luncheon was announced.

"It's a terrible story, Mr. Ashfold, but we mustn't let it spoil our luncheon. Give me your arm to the dining-room, and let us lay in a little stock of strength before entering on the discussion of that formidable business. Culwarren, are you taking care of our dear Lily? But I need scarcely have put the question. Ah, Mr. Ashfold, I expect we shall have to draw largely on your services before long, to take rather a heavy responsibility in the shape of drawing up the marriage settlements for the future Countess of Culwarren."

"Indeed, my lady! Is his lordship, then, thinking of taking the irretrievable plunge so early?"

"Hush! Not so loud. It is a secret, for the present at all events, but I have no doubt that it will be public property before long."

"Exactly so. Odd, isn't it? People *will* marry. Never did it myself, but find other people do. Exactly so."

In another minute the whole company were seated round the luncheon-table, busily engaged in discussing the meal set before them. Lord Culwarren had secured a seat next Lily Osprey, and was trying hard to extract some answer from her to his impassioned whispers. The guests were making their private comments on the evident distinction made by the Countess between her two sons. Miss Paget was pretending to do the honours of the table, but with all her thoughts evidently far away, and Lady Culwarren was animadverting to Mr. Ashfold on the iniquities of the Honourable Anthony Melstrom, when the door was thrown open by the powdered flunkey, and the gentleman in question was loudly announced. The intelligence had a varied effect upon the assembly. The visitors looked eagerly expectant to see the younger son of whom they had heard such different accounts. Lord Culwarren started anxiously from his seat, and his mother's brow became dark and lowering. But nothing seemed to influence the behaviour of the joyous Anthony, who burst into the room with the impetuosity of a liberated schoolboy, and going straight up to the Countess, saluted her warmly on the cheek.

"My dear Anthony," she exclaimed, with more surprise than pleasure, "is this really *you*?"

"My dear mother," he echoed, "it really *is*. I suppose you received my letter this morning, and it is all right, but I could not wait a moment longer to see you all again. Ah, Culwarren, my dear fellow," he continued, shaking hands vehemently with his brother, "how are you? Still determined to be a genius, eh? I saw the advertisement of something or other, with your name attached to it, in the paper to-day. And, Miss Paget, you have not quite forgotten your troublesome charge, I hope, for I have never forgotten you!"

And then he arrived at Lily, and his joyous voice fell at once to a tender undertone, as he looked at the lovely, blushing face, and the dark eyes swimming with tears, that dare not look at him again.

"And this is my cousin Lily," he said, as he took her hand in his. He appeared to have had a long sentence on his tongue with which to greet her, but the words died away as if by magic, and he could only hold her hand and be silent.

CHAPTER VII

STARTLING INTELLIGENCE.

HIS action, so evident to all the company, nettled Lady Culwarren in the extreme.

" Anthony," she called, sharply, "you forget that I have not introduced you to my guests."

At that she ran over the names of all present rapidly, ending with the announcement, " My son, Mr. Melstrom."

" And now come and sit by me," she continued, "and explain why you have taken us all by surprise in this way. If you had had a little patience, the carriage would have fetched you. It was ordered to start directly after luncheon."

" But, my dear mother, you forget that to a man in my position the minutes drag like hours. How could I sit down to exercise patience (with which I was never overstocked) when my heart was longing to see you all again? Why, I have been looking out for that carriage ever since breakfast, and so I resolved to walk over and send it back for my friend Fosbrooke." And again his eyes travelled in the direction of Lily's figure and settled there.

"You have not spoken to Mr. Ashfold," recommenced the Countess; "surely you must remember him."

"Really, I am afraid I do not. Stay, though, I am wronging myself; I do remember. You were my dear father's legal adviser, were you not?" said Anthony, as he tendered his hand to Ashfold.

"Your *father*? Exactly so," replied the solicitor, in a vague manner; "and you are twenty-one to-day, sir. A fine-grown young man of his age, my lady."

"Oh, yes! Mr. Melstrom was always *big*," remarked Lady Culwarren, as though his qualifications began and ended with the circumstance. Yet she could not help glancing enviously—almost spitefully, indeed—at his improved looks, and stature, and bearing. His brother, the Earl, presented a sorry figure when seated next to him, and so, with one accord, appeared to think the guests of Gardenholme. Many a furtive look of admiration was cast in the direction of the handsome young fellow, who had no eyes for any one but his cousin Lily, and whose wandering attention had constantly to be recalled to what his mother or Ashfold said to him. It was gall and wormwood to her to perceive the interest excited by her despised younger son, and she wished in her heart of hearts that he had not appeared at so inauspicious a moment.

"And so you are all going on in the same old grooves, I suppose?" exclaimed Anthony, lightly, when Lily's crimson cheeks had warned him not to look her way any longer, "and with no changes except in the names of the days of the week. I'm afraid the routine of an English country life will appear rather monotonous to me after the stirring scenes in which I have mixed abroad."

"Excuse me, Anthony," said Lady Culwarren,

in her coldest tone, "but we are likely to see important changes here before long."

"Indeed! I am glad of it for your sake, though I should be sorry to see any radical alteration in the appearance of my dear old home. *That*, at all events, can never be improved. By the way, my dear mother, I am most anxious to present my friend Fosbrooke to you. He knew my father in his bachelor days, and I am sure you will all like him exceedingly."

"Any friend of yours will of course be welcome, Anthony," replied the Countess, with careless indifference.

"I knew you would say that, mother, and wanted him to walk over with me this morning in consequence, but he refused to come without an invitation from yourself; so may I trouble you to write a little note to him, to go with the carriage to Dearham?"

"Certainly. Miss Paget, be good enough to write to Mr. Fosbrooke in my name, and invite him to stay at Gardenholme."

"You will find him the most delightful

companion that it is possible to have," continued Anthony, enthusiastically. "Though I have only known him for a month, I regard him as my best friend. He knows everything, and has been everywhere. He hunts, shoots, sings, plays billiards, tennis, and cards; can stalk or walk or ride; in fact, there is nothing he cannot do. And to crown it all, under an assumed cynicism, he possesses the warmest heart alive."

"An Admirable Crichton," said Miss Paget, with something like a sneer.

"Ah, Miss Paget! I recognise that tone of old. You were always a disbeliever in the virtues of our poor sex. Has time made no difference in your opinions? Won't you make a little concession in favour of my friend?"

"Opinions that can be altered by time are not usually worth much to begin with, Mr. Melstrom."

"How dare you call me 'Mr. Melstrom'? I— who was once your little 'Tony,' and whom you kissed at parting. Oh, Miss Paget, if that is one of the changes time will effect, I shall begin to run down its merits at once."

The companion smiled faintly at his rally, but she did not answer it, and Lady Culwarren, perceiving the meal was concluded, gave the signal for dispersion by rising from the table.

"Come, Culwarren," exclaimed young Melstrom, as he linked his arm in that of his brother, "show me the new conservatory and the billiard-room, of which I have heard so much, before Fosbrooke arrives, for after that contingency takes place I shall not receive much attention from anybody. Come, Lily, I have seen nothing of you yet! I cannot spare you on the first day of my return."

He extended his hand to his cousin as he spoke, and she glanced towards her aunt and coloured painfully.

" Stay, Anthony," exclaimed Lady Culwarren ; "you cannot have everything your own way without even consulting the wishes of others. *I* may require the attendance of my niece during our afternoon drive."

" Has your ladyship forgotten the object of my visit? My business is of the utmost import-ance and cannot wait," observed the solicitor, who was standing by. The Countess knit her brows with vexation.

"How annoying! What am I to do? I cannot have Lily running all over the place with that wild boy," she murmured to Miss Paget.

"Lord Culwarren will be with them," replied the companion.

"Of course! Thanks for the reminder. Lily, my dear, you can go with your cousins since they desire it. And, Culwarren, bring her back to me in half an hour's time. I have some business with Mr. Ashfold which will detain me until then," said the Countess, significantly. But Anthony saw nothing but Lily's blushing face, and drew her triumphantly from the room.

"Wild and boisterous as ever," sighed Lady Culwarren, as the door closed upon them. "Anthony never had any manners, and he never will have any. His foreign travel has not improved him a bit!"

"Are you not a little hard on him?" asked Miss Paget. "You should make some allowance for his youth. Experience and the world are sure to tame him by-and-by."

"Meanwhile, we are to be inconvenienced by his want of politeness. What can my guests have thought of the bearishness of my younger son? He has scarcely spoken a word to any of them."

"Remember he has only just returned home."

"I am not likely to forget it, Miss Paget. I only wish he had stayed away for another six months. And what induced him to bring his cosmopolitan friend to Gardenholme? He knows how conservative I am, and how I detest anything that approaches Bohemianism."

"That reminds me I must write the note you desired me to send with the carriage for Mr. Fosbrooke."

"Please be quick about it, then, for I want you to attend me in the library, where I am about to talk business with Mr. Ashfold."

"May I suggest," interposed the lawyer, "that my business with your ladyship is strictly private and confidential, and that I hoped, in consequence, to have seen you by yourself?"

The Countess raised her painted eyebrows in surprise at his audacity.

"I have no secrets from Miss Paget, Mr. Ashfold, and I prefer that she should be present at our interview."

The little man reddened to his ears at this rebuke, but merely shrugged his shoulders as he replied :

"Certainly—most certainly, since your lady-ship wishes it, and very natural you should wish it, too, perhaps. Still, you will not forget that I suggested a strictly private interview."

"I don't wish for any of your suggestions," said Lady Culwarren, curtly. "Come, Miss Paget."

Miss Paget, who had hastily scribbled the note of invitation at a side table, and given it into the charge of a servant, was not at all surprised at the Countess's decision, for ever since the death of her husband, Lady Culwarren had almost entirely depended on her companion for guidance in her business and household matters, which Miss Paget, being not only a lady by birth and education, but a far more intellectual woman than her employer, was well fitted to bestow. And the Countess had gone even farther than that; she had made Miss Paget an intimate friend and counsellor, and would have felt lost had she not been always at her elbow, to give her good advice and help her put it into execution.

"And now, Mr. Ashfold," exclaimed Lady Culwarren, as, having gained the library, she sank down on a sofa and made her companion take a seat beside her, "I am ready to hear the reason of your unexpected visit to us to-day."

The solicitor looked from one lady to the other with a jerky motion of the head like an inquisitive crow.

"Exactly so, and I am perfectly aware that your ladyship holds Miss Paget in the highest esteem and closest friendship. Still, if I may venture to repeat what I said just now, without offending you, this is a matter of a very private and confidential nature indeed."

The Countess drew herself up in an offended manner.

"No, Mr. Ashfold, you may *not* repeat it. I cannot conceive it possible that you have anything to say to me but what Miss Paget is quite welcome to hear. She knows all about our property, investments, and estates, and before Culwarren came of age was my most valued adviser, and if there is anything further for her to learn, I am quite willing she should hear it."

"It must be as your ladyship wishes, of course, but you seem to forget there may be family secrets which have nothing whatever to do with property or estates. Do not blame me, therefore, if in the course of our conversation I should make disclosures which you would rather have kept to yourself."

"Gracious heavens, Mr. Ashfold, you make me feel quite nervous! What awful story are you about to disclose, and to whom does it refer?"

"Exactly so. I was sure that was the first question you would put to me. But we mustn't go too fast; we must take our time about it."

"I am sure you needn't be afraid of using too much expedition, Mr. Ashfold. You are always terribly slow, and you don't seem inclined to hurry yourself on this occasion."

"Exactly so. Mine is a slow profession, my

lady. But my intelligence must be preceded by a little explanation. The instructions, then, upon which I am now acting I have had by me for a long time—indeed, ever since the late Earl's death, ten years ago. Amongst his papers I found a sealed packet addressed to me, and marked *Private*, and not to be opened till the 15th of August in the present year—that is to-day."

"How very strange!" remarked the Countess. "Miss Paget, I know you were in the confidence of my late husband. Did he at any time mention such a packet to you?"

"Never, Lady Culwarren."

"Nor to me. It seems curious, if he had any private directions to leave behind, that he did not address them to *me*—his wife."

"Exactly so. But pardon me, my lady, the packet was to be kept unopened for ten years, and do you think, under the circumstances, that you would have had the patience to carry out his lordship's directions?"

"Ah, well! there's no saying. It would have been a trying position. But let us hear what you

found when you *did* open it. No second family,
I hope, or anything unpleasant of that sort."

"No, indeed! Pray do not alarm yourself.
Yesterday, the 14th, I was summoned, as I have
told you, to Sir Hugh Loftus, and brought the
packet with me, guessing that it must relate to
this estate, and I might have to come here at
once. When I awoke this morning, the 15th of
August, I opened the packet."

"Now you are getting prosy," cried Lady
Culwarren. "We all know that it is the 15th
of August. Why need you be so precise?"

"Mine is a precise profession, my lady."

"Well, well, do make haste now. What does
the packet contain?"

"It contains certain information, Lady Culwarren, with respect to a young gentleman known
in society as the Honourable Anthony Melstrom."

At these words both of the ladies looked considerably alarmed, though from different causes.
The Countess started violently, and changed
colour even through her rouge. She feared the
news might affect the interests of her beloved

son Culwarren. But Miss Paget grew paler than her wont, for she loved the reckless younger son better than any of the family, and she dreaded to see him stripped, perhaps, of the small possession he could call his own.

" To Anthony?" exclaimed Lady Culwarren, when she had somewhat recovered herself. " What of him? Surely it can be nothing to the detriment of the Earl?"

" To the detriment of the Earl!" repeated Mr. Ashfold. " Very natural alarm. Exactly so. Oh, no, there is nothing here that can possibly affect the interests of Lord Culwarren."

" Neither can I imagine that any intelligence deferred until his twenty-first birthday can have any power to injure the Honourable Anthony Melstrom," interposed Miss Paget, in her hard and constrained voice.

The little solicitor, who was fumbling in his black bag for the document in question, turned and regarded her with the same keen, searching gaze he had bestowed on her in the drawing-room. But Miss Paget, who had drawn closer to the Countess and taken her hand, as though to support her under any coming struggle, did not appear to notice his scrutiny.

" Exactly so. A little patience and you shall know all. Lady Culwarren and Miss Paget, you are both women of the world. You have probably heard and seen strange things in your time, and will not be overmuch startled at any intelligence. Still, the information contained in this packet, and which I am instructed to impart to you, my lady, is sufficient to startle any one. It is that the Honourable Anthony Melstrom (so-called) *is not your son.*"

"Anthony not my son!" repeated the Countess, incredulously. "Mr. Ashfold! You must be dreaming."

"I never dream, my lady. I haven't the time. But I knew you would accuse me of something of the sort."

"Not my son!" said Lady Culwarren again, in a mystified voice. "It is impossible!"

"Mr. Ashfold," interposed Miss Paget, with much agitation, "pray think of what you are saying! Think of the awful injury your assertion entails upon him."

"I can't help that, madam. I did not write this paper, nor did I know anything before to-day of the antecedents of the gentleman in question."

"Not my son!" reiterated the Countess, but without any apparent feeling except disbelief. "You are a bold man, Mr. Ashfold, to tell a mother to her face that the child she brought into the world is not her own."

"There must be some terrible mistake," said her companion.

"Exactly so. Just what I should have said myself, perhaps, but I cannot deny the truth of his lordship's written testimony."

"Oh, go on! Go on, and let us hear all," cried Lady Culwarren, with feverish anxiety. "No, Miss Paget, thank you, I need no support. I am very much astonished, I confess, and very incredulous, but I do not feel at all ill. Pray do not keep me any longer in suspense, Mr. Ashfold, but let me know at once all that my late husband says upon the subject."

CHAPTER VIII.

WHO IS ANTHONY?

"YOU must bear in mind, my lady," continued the solicitor, "that I was not the late Earl's legal adviser at the time of his marriage with yourself, and was therefore unacquainted with a certain family history—a very sad history, indeed, that occurred just before that event."

"I understand what you allude to, Mr. Ashfold —that disgraceful affair concerning his sister, Lady Diana Melstrom, and which threatened at one time to put a stop to our marriage. The Fairleys have always been most circumspect in their behaviour, and my people didn't think it at all nice that I should become connected with a person of that sort. Miss Paget, the news about this foolish boy has positively affected you more

than it has me. You have turned quite pale.
Now I must insist upon your resuming your seat
and keeping yourself quiet. It would be a pretty
ending to this matter if you made yourself ill.
Now, Mr. Ashfold, it seems that this unfortunate
lady fell in love with some man, whose name Lord
Culwarren has purposely refrained from stating,
and I have no means by which to ascertain."

"If his lordship *purposely* refrained from stating
it, I should think you had no right to *try* and
ascertain," said the companion, slowly.

"Exactly so. Just what I should have said
myself. Whoever he was, however, he seems to
have been a wild, harum-scarum fellow, and probably of inferior birth to her ladyship. Anyway,
Lord Culwarren would not hear of the connection,
and Lady Diana, who was a self-willed and
thoughtless girl, took the law into her own hands
and eloped with this nameless admirer."

"Shameless creature!" exclaimed the Countess,
emphatically; "so inconsiderate for all related to
her. I have no patience with such women. They
should be condemned to penal servitude for life."

"Exactly so. Perhaps they get it," said Mr. Ashfold.

"But what has Lady Diana's escapade to do with Anthony?" continued Lady Culwarren. "We hoped that the world had forgotten all about that long ago. She ran away with her lover—married him—and died—and there was an end of her story."

"I am coming to it fast, my lady. Lady Diana died, but have you ever heard in what manner? She believed that the man she married was at least an honourable one, but she was mistaken. Her union with him was an empty ceremony, for shortly afterwards she found he was already married to some intriguing adventuress, and returning home, threw herself, broken-hearted, on her brother's mercy."

"I have heard all this—at least, in outline. But she was the late Earl's favourite sister, and he was very unwilling to talk about her. He said the best thing we could all do was to forget the poor girl had ever existed. He would never even tell me where she was buried. Miss Paget, please don't fidget with those windows. There is quite enough air in the room already."

" Perhaps Miss Paget feels faint," remarked Mr. Ashfold, as he went to her assistance.

" Not at all, thank you," replied the companion ; " I only thought the weather very oppressive. But if Lady Culwarren does not wish this window opened, I will take a seat by the further one."

" One would never imagine," observed her ladyship, fretfully, " that we had met to discuss a subject of vital importance to me and to my children, by the absurd way in which you two people are keeping me in suspense, whilst you decide whether to raise a window-sash or keep it down."

" Pardon me, my lady," replied Mr. Ashfold, hastily, " but I feared the heat of the day was becoming too much for Miss Paget. To resume business, then, on the 15th of August, twenty-one years ago, you had a son born."

" Of course I had — my son, Anthony Melstrom. Every one who was about me at the time knows the fact as well as myself."

"Exactly so. At least, you think they do. You may remember that you were very ill with fever on that occasion, and delirious for weeks."

"I know I was. But what of that?"

"Your life was despaired of, my lady, and your child died."

"My child died! Why, Anthony is that child. You must be raving, Mr. Ashfold."

"Exactly so. I mean, quite the contrary. When they began to entertain hopes of your recovery, the doctors feared you might have a relapse if informed of your infant's death, and they advised that another child of about the same age should be substituted for yours."

"Oh, this is incredible," cried the Countess; "his lordship must have been out of his mind when he invented such a fable."

"These papers, Lady Culwarren, bear no impress of a wandering mind. The story is told in a plain, straightforward manner, and the statement is regularly signed and witnessed. No unprejudiced reader could doubt its entire truth."

"Somebody else's child was substituted for my dead son, and I was never informed of it? If this be true, I have been made the subject of a gross and unpardonable fraud."

"It was done to help your recovery, my lady. Whether his lordship acted wisely in concealing the fact from you altogether, it is not my business to determine. I have done my duty in announcing it to you now."

"But will you be good enough to tell me, then, whose son I have been bringing up in place of the Honourable Mr. Melstrom, Mr. Ashfold?"

"Ah, Lady Culwarren, whose son? That's the puzzle. My instructions on this point are not so accurate as I could wish them to be. I have my surmises, of course. My profession does not prohibit me from surmising; but there is no certainty. Only since the late Earl has thought fit to provide for this young man by his will, and to desire that he shall continue to bear the family name, I think we shall not be far wrong in concluding that Mr. Anthony Melstrom is some connection of his own."

"And I am determined to find out who he may be," exclaimed the Countess, angrily; "I have never taken to that boy from his very infancy, and the want of affection I have felt for him should have warned me he was not my own flesh and blood. But I decline any longer to be made responsible, even for friendship, towards a young man who may have sprung from the lowest of the low."

"Your ladyship will, I trust, do nothing rashly," interposed the lawyer. "Whoever the lad may be, the late Earl evidently regarded him as an especial *protégé*."

"And he had his own reasons for doing so, doubtless," retorted the Countess, shrilly; "and these reasons I shall not rest until I have discovered. Miss Paget, you were not with us at the time of Anthony's birth, but you may have heard my husband mention this dishonourable transaction. Did he ever tell you that the boy was not *my* son, or hint at his real parentage before you?"

"*Never! Indeed*," replied Miss Paget, emphatically, "this intelligence is as startling and as incredible to me as to yourself, Lady Culwarren, and I find it quite impossible to believe it. Mr. Melstrom not your son! Why, he bears the Christian name of the late Earl, and always appeared to be his favourite of the two! Besides, is he not supposed to be the image of his late grandfather? Several of the family have remarked the likeness to me."

"Of course he is," replied Lady Culwarren, bitterly, for the admiration conferred upon the younger son had ever been an annoyance to her. "He is exactly like the portraits of the old Lord Culwarren, who was hated for his vices by the entire county. It is said that it was his harshness and ill-temper that drove Lady Diana to take the fatal step she did. But Mr. Melstrom is not a bit like me, and for that reason I am resolved to search this matter to the bottom. I will have none of the late Earl's indiscretions foisted on Culwarren and myself for affection or patronage. Ring the bell, Miss Paget, if you please, and summon Mrs. Matthews."

"Exactly so," acquiesced Mr. Ashfold, who was sorry for the awkward turn the Countess's suspicions had taken; "but who is Mrs. Matthews? We must not bruit this little matter abroad more than is absolutely necessary, Lady Culwarren."

"I believe I know *les convenances* as well as most people, Mr. Ashfold," replied her lady-ship, stiffly, "and am as little likely to transgress them. Mrs. Matthews' position in Gardenholme at present is a sinecure, but she was nurse to my late husband, and has been in the family ever since. If any person living is acquainted with the parentage of Anthony Melstrom, that person will be Mrs. Matthews. Please send for her at once." And then the three sat very silent and uncomfortable, awaiting the advent of the servant in their midst. She was a domestic of the old stamp—the stamp that is worn out, effaced, almost forgotten. Summoned from her snug sitting-room on the ground-floor of the Abbey, she made a profound obeisance as she entered the library. She was an old woman of perhaps seventy summers, but she was as upright as a dart, and had piercing

eyes like an eagle. She wore a black stuff
dress and a large black silk apron, and had a
white muslin kerchief quaintly pinned across her
bosom. Her high, well-starched cap with its
bow of black ribbon formed a subject of ridicule
for all the fine ladies'-maids who visited Gardenholme; but Mrs. Matthews regarded the servants
of the present day with ill-disguised contempt,
and retained the same fashion in dress in which
she had dandled the late Earl of Culwarren fifty
years before. She advanced to the table at which
the Countess and the lawyer were seated, and
though Lady Culwarren requested the old woman
more than once to take a chair, she remained
standing throughout the interview, and would have
dropped from fatigue sooner than commit the
sacrilege of sitting down in the presence of
her superiors.

"Mr. Ashfold has come down to Gardenholme
to-day to convey some very strange intelligence
to me, Mrs. Matthews," commenced the Countess.

"Indeed, my lady?"

"Something which *you* must know more about

than anybody else living, and I have sent for you, in order that you may enlighten us."

Miss Paget vacated her seat by the window, and drawing nearer to the table, looked up in the old servant's face with the greatest anxiety. She was not singular in taking an interest in Anthony Melstrom's fortunes. Every one who knew him loved the lad—except the woman who had hitherto believed herself to be his mother.

"If there is any information I can give your ladyship," commenced Mrs. Matthews, deferentially.

"Shall I break the news to her?" demanded Ashfold.

"I prefer to do it myself," said Lady Culwarren, quickly. "Mrs. Matthews, you knew my husband from infancy, and have lived with me ever since my marriage. Answer me truly. Whose child is Anthony Melstrom?"

At this sudden and unexpected attack, the old servant's presence of mind seemed entirely to desert her. She clasped her palsied hands together and could scarcely articulate from alarm.

" *Whose* child, my lady ? " she reiterated, after
a pause. " Why, your child, surely. Didn't you
bring him into the world this very day twenty-one
years ago, God bless him ? Dear, dear, whose
child should he be but yours ? "

"That's just what I want you to tell me, Mrs.
Matthews. Of course, I thought until to-day
that he was, as you say, my son; but Mr.
Ashfold informs me that your master left a paper
behind him to certify that he is *not*."

" Exactly so," asserted the solicitor. " A
perfectly legal document, Mrs. Matthews, signed
sealed, and witnessed, to say that the Countess's
son died shortly after his birth, and this boy was
substituted in his place. This news has naturally
much upset her ladyship, and so, if you know
anything about the affair, you can do no harm
by telling it, as the secret is out, and no mistake.
Exactly so."

Mrs. Matthews turned her gaze alternately
from the Countess to the lawyer, and from the
lawyer to the companion, with a face of the
deepest distress.

"Don't let the news upset you like this," said Miss Paget, kindly, as she laid one hand on the old woman's shaking frame. "We know you must feel it—everybody will feel it — Mr. Melstrom is such a general favourite. But the Earl has provided for him in his will, and it is only right that the truth should be made known at last. The error has been in withholding it so long."

"And my dear master has left a paper to say that blessed boy is not his own?" exclaimed Mrs. Matthews, incredulously.

"Oh, no, Matthews. You quite mistake," interrupted the Countess, in a sarcastic voice; "the document only affirms that Anthony Melstrom is not *my* son."

The old servant was sharp enough to perceive the implied alternative.

"Humbly begging your pardon, my lady," she said, "I knew my lord long before you did. I dandled him as an infant in my arms, and you're doing him a wrong by your suspicion. He was good and true from first to last. If he brought

another person's child into this house and passed
it off as yours, it was to save your life and reason,
and not for any base purpose of his own. You
may take my word for that."

"Come, then, Mrs. Matthews, you *do* know
something about this business, that is very evident,
and I must beg you to tell me what it is," replied
Lady Culwarren. "I will not be deceived any
longer, you may depend upon that, and the more
you can convince me that your words are true,
the better it will be for Mr. Melstrom."

Miss Paget pressed the old woman's hand.
" Have courage, Matthews," she whispered, "and
tell all you know."

The servant looked in her anxious face com-
passionately.

" If I dared," she began, and then suddenly
turned to Mr. Ashfold.

" Mayn't I know what's in the paper, sir ? "

" Certainly," replied Ashfold, and he reiterated
what he had confided to Lady Culwarren.

" Well, then, my lady," said the woman, " it's
no use holding my tongue any longer. What the

Earl says there is true. Mr. Anthony is not your son."

"But whose son is he ?"

"That's more than I can tell you, my lady. I remember your terrible illness well. Day and night I watched with the Earl by your bedside, and I thought he would have gone mad as well as yourself, for he was bowed down with terrible grief and shame the while. It was weeks before the fever bettered and you came to yourself again, and all that time you had been raving about your baby, and saying you had killed it, and would be had up for murder. So the doctor said, whatever we did afterwards, we *must* get an infant for you to fondle when you first recovered your senses."

"I have heard all that," rejoined the Countess, coldly, "and the unpardonable trick that was played on me. You are certain that my child *died*?"

"Oh, yes, my lady; pretty dear! that it did, for I put it in its coffin with my own hands, and his lordship was terribly cut up about it too. And if you was to make search in the family vault, you'd

find the little coffin without ever a name on, for it
didn't live to be baptized. And that's Gospel
truth."

"But, Mrs. Matthews, I must have more.
Where did Anthony come from?"

"I can't tell you, my lady."

"Whose child is he?"

"I can't tell you that either, my lady. If my
master had known it himself, wouldn't he have
written it down?"

"That's nonsense. He *must* have known it.
Who brought the child to Gardenholme?"

"The medical gentleman, my lady, whom his
lordship deputed to fetch it."

"And you mean me to believe, Matthews, that
you never even asked *whose* baby it was—nor any
of the other servants? You all saw a strange
infant brought and put in the place of my poor
dead child, and you had not even the curiosity to
inquire *who* were its parents, nor *where* it came
from? I don't believe it. The virtue of discretion
is too rare."

"But pardon me, my lady, none of the other

servants knew anything of the matter. As soon
as it was evident that his own poor dear baby
must die, his lordship made his arrangements
accordingly."

"He went out and found the Honourable
Anthony Melstrom under a hedge, I suppose,"
sneered the Countess. "I repeat that I have been
shamefully duped and deceived."

"I cannot tell your ladyship where he found
him. It was no part of my duty to pry into my
master's secrets. All I know is that he brought
him home and laid him in my arms, and told me
to treat him as if he were his son. And I'm sure
if your own dear baby had lived, my lady, he
couldn't have grown into a finer, handsomer, nor
more loving young gentleman than Mr. Anthony."

"Hush! Pray do not treat me to any of this
nonsense. If his lordship wished me to treat the
young man with any consideration, he should have
kept this disgraceful secret to himself. Well,
Mr. Ashfold, we seem no nearer the solution of the
mystery. This old woman cannot, or will not,
give us the least clue to the parentage of

Mr. Melstrom, and so the only conclusion that I can arrive at is, that my husband palmed off on my protection some base-born child of his own."

"No, no, my lady, I *know* that is not the case," exclaimed Mrs. Matthews.

"Will your ladyship permit me to ask one or two questions of her?" said the lawyer, persuasively. "You were surprised, perhaps, at my dwelling so much just now on the history of Lady Diana Melstrom. Exactly so. But I had my reasons. You seem agitated, Mrs. Matthews. You knew Lady Diana, of course, and are acquainted with the events I allude to?"

"*Knew her*, sir! Why, didn't I nurse her from the day of her birth, and love her like my own child? She was ten years younger than the Earl. God rest them both!"

"Very creditable! Very creditable, indeed!" remarked Mr. Ashfold. "Now, attention, please, Mrs. Matthews, and don't attempt any prevarication. Are you, or are you not, prepared to say that Mr. Anthony is not the son of Lady Diana Melstrom?"

CHAPTER IX.

THE COMPANION.

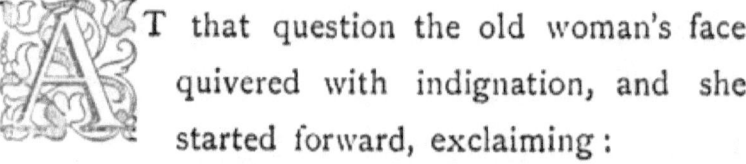T that question the old woman's face quivered with indignation, and she started forward, exclaiming :

"Oh, sir ! For shame ! for shame ! You have no right to make so cruel and groundless an assertion concerning my dear dead mistress."

And then she sat down in the chair which she had refused to occupy, and, hiding her face behind her withered palm, began to cry feebly.

"Mrs. Matthews," said Lady Culwarren, majestically, "I am surprised at your presumption in addressing Mr. Ashfold in such a manner. You forget yourself."

"Oh, pardon, pardon, my lady !" replied the servant, in a quavering tone ; "but to the dead ! It is so cruel—so cruel !"

"I cannot say that I quite see the cruelty of it myself," remarked the lawyer, "and it is an important factor in the chain of events. Lady Diana believed herself to be a married woman. No one would dream of imputing a particle of blame to her, poor thing. It was her misfortune, not her fault. But I have been making some inquiries lately, and I find there is no doubt that, after returning to the protection of her brother, she gave birth to a child, a circumstance which the Earl, in order to save his sister's reputation and the name of the family, desired, most naturally, to conceal from the knowledge of the world. He therefore, so I understand, bribed her attendants to persuade her that the infant was stillborn, and had it conveyed away to be reared at his own expense. Soon afterwards Lady Diana Melstrom is said to have died — in Rome, I believe, or Florence. What more probable, then, that finding a child was necessary to ensure your ladyship's restoration to health, the Earl should have brought his nephew to be substituted in place of his son? The dates of birth are within a month of one another, and I feel no doubt on the matter myself. Exactly so——"

But here a deep sigh — almost more like a moan than a sigh — was borne upon the still summer air, and Mr. Ashfold's attention was directed to the companion.

" Good gracious ! Mrs. Matthews, look after Miss Paget ; she is fainting. I told your ladyship the temperature of this room was too high for her—or for anybody, in fact, except a visitor from the infernal regions," he muttered to himself. But both the women were too much occupied with Miss Paget to heed what he said.

"Do make yourself of some use," cried the Countess, impatiently, as she supported the head of her companion. " Get a fan, or ring the bell for some water, or do something. It's all your business that has brought on this attack, Mr. Ashfold. You might have told your story in half the time. Get my smelling-salts, Mrs. Matthews; you will find them on the writing-table. Dear me ! she looks very white and drawn. What can have occasioned this sudden illness?"

"Let me take her to her own room, my lady," pleaded the old woman, who was trembling violently. "I have often seen her in these attacks before, and she will be terribly upset when she comes to herself if she finds she is not quite alone."

"Quite alone! What nonsense, when she is my dearest friend! Perhaps it would be better if Mr. Ashfold were to leave us, but Miss Paget cannot possibly have any objection to my presence, who am more like a sister to her than anything else."

"I know you are, my lady, and so does she, poor thing. Many's the time she has spoken to me of your goodness and kindness to her. But pray let her be carried to her room. She's gone off just like death, and she will recover nowhere so well as on her own bed. I beg your ladyship to order the servants to carry her upstairs."

In the face of this entreaty on the part of Mrs. Matthews, who was considered quite an authority on medical matters in the household, Lady Cul-warren did not like to hold out any longer, and so assistance was procured, and accompanied by the old servant, the unconscious form of the companion was conveyed to the upper landing, whilst the Countess, offended at having been forced to give way against her will, prepared to discuss with Mr. Ashfold the best course of conduct to pursue with regard to Anthony Melstrom.

Meantime, Miss Paget having been placed on her bed, was left (excepting for the presence of Mrs. Matthews) alone. As soon as the other servants had quitted the apartment, the old woman carefully locked the door behind them and busied herself in restoring her charge. She loosened the fastenings of the black dress she wore, disclosing a neck and shoulders of alabaster fairness; then she removed the mob-cap which hid the companion's wealth of hair, and let the pale-golden tresses, flecked here and there with gray, flow over the pillow on which she lay. Viewed in this light, Miss Paget appeared what she really was—a beautiful though prematurely aged woman of nine-

and-thirty—beautiful, that is to say, so far as well-formed features went ; but the beauty of colour and expression — the beauty that comes with happiness—the beauty, in fact, of life, had all been washed out of her face by some great trouble or anxiety. She lay on her bed like a marble statue, without hope or feeling, but fixed, re-signed, immovable. Mrs. Matthews continued to bathe her forehead with eau - de - cologne, and hold the smelling-salts to her nostrils, and more than once during her task did she stoop to kiss her hands or silken hair, murmuring half-broken sentences of pity or affection the while. At last the companion opened her eyes, dreamily and wonderingly at first, as people are accustomed to do after a swoon ; but as they fell upon the servant, and she watched the officiousness with which she attended on her, remembrance seemed suddenly to flash upon her mind, and she started up with a wild look of terror.

"What is it? What is it?" she exclaimed. "Have they found me out? Does that man know me?"

"No, no, my dearie," replied the old nurse, soothingly; "no one said nothing of the kind. Now do lie again and rest a little. You're not fit to leave your bed yet awhile. Lie down, as your old nursie tells you."

And she attempted to force her back to a recumbent posture, but she might as well have tried to control the dead.

"Stay," cried Miss Paget, suddenly; "I can remember now. They spoke of *Anthony*."

Then she turned to the old servant and clutched her shoulder like a vice.

"Matthews, tell me the truth, as if you and I were standing before the judgment seat of God. Did that man lie, or is Anthony Melstrom the child which you told me never breathed?"

"Oh, my dear lady, what shall I say to you?"

"The truth, and nothing but the truth. I know you know it, and I will *kill* you, but you shall tell it me."

She looked dangerous in her passionate suspense with the mother-love gleaming hungrily from her eyes, and the old woman cowered before her.

"But I *swore*," she gasped. "I took a solemn oath to the Earl and before high Heaven that I would keep the secret until I died. Oh, my lady, you won't ask me to forswear myself?"

"But he never dreamt that others would hint the truth before me, and raise this demon of anxiety in my breast. Matthews, I absolve you, in the name of my dead brother, from your oath. It concerns me more than anybody else. For God's sake, tell me the truth."

"I cannot refuse you, my lady. Mr. Anthony is your child. I took him, by my lord's orders, from your side myself, and my own sister kept him until he was brought to Gardenholme and exchanged for the dead baby of Lady Culwarren. But it was by his lordship's orders, my dear. Pray remember that, and I believed with him, as there's a heaven above us, that it was the best thing for your honour and happiness."

But Miss Paget did not appear to have heard her last words. She leapt from the bed and

commenced walking up and down the room, like
a creature possessed, throwing her arms about and
laughing and weeping by turns.

"My child!" she exclaimed, hysterically, "my
child. How did they *dare* to tell me you were
dead, my living, breathing child? My Anthony.
Ah! who can wonder now that I have been drawn
as no other creature has ever had the power to
draw me? It was the strength of motherhood,
mighty even in unconsciousness. Anthony *mine*.
My boy, my son. My own, *own* child. Matthews!"
she continued, as she observed the old servant's
stricken attitude, "don't be afraid, but tell me
everything. I forgive you all your share in this
transaction. I am sure you did it for the best.
I feel as if I could forgive everybody, because
I am so happy in the knowledge that he lives
—so very, very happy, that I could even bless
the bitter teaching of the past."

"Oh, my dear lady, *what* will come of all
this?"

"I do not know. I cannot think. I can remember only one thing—that he is *mine*. Oh,

Matthews! how had you the heart to take him from me, when you saw how I needed the comfort I should have had in him?"

"It nearly broke my heart, my lady, it did indeed—but, as I said just now, I thought I was doing the kindest thing by you, to save you from more shame and sorrow than you needed to bear. And when his lordship, after some years, brought you back from Rome to live here with his countess, he bound me by that solemn oath never to reveal to you that Mr. Melstrom was your son, and may he forgive me for doing it now. But I've seen your love for him, my lady, and watched your secret sorrows, and my heart has bled for you. It has, indeed."

"And I believe it, Matthews. I believe, too, that my brother Culwarren meant it for the best; but it was a cruel kindness. A mother's rights should be unalienable. God gives them to her, God only should have the power to retake them. I see now why Culwarren brought me back to Gardenholme, and placed me under a false name in my own family and beside *my son*. How often did he, when dying, beseech me to love and cherish Anthony? Oh! it is joy beyond telling to know my darling lives. And yet," with a sudden pang, "never to acknowledge him—never to hear his dear voice call me 'Mother'! Oh, Matthews, how shall I endure it?"

"Hush, hush! my dear lady. You have been so brave and borne so much without complaint. Don't let your stout heart fail you now."

"But I did not know then that Anthony was my child. I believed I had no one in the world either to love or to live for. But now, to dwell in his presence—to hear his happy voice, to watch his dear, bright face—to hear others praising and admiring him, and never to be able to tell them *he is mine*—oh, Heaven, help me! The weary years that I have passed in silent, hopeless agony have dwindled down to nothing beside this. My punishment has but just descended on my head." And throwing herself prostrate on the bed, the unhappy woman burst into a flood of tears. Mrs. Matthews became alarmed.

"My dear, you will never betray yourself now,

surely. What good could it lead to? Think of
your noble brother lying in his grave, and the
pains he took to conceal it. Think of your honour
and that of the family. And poor Master Anthony,
too. What would become of us all if you were
to disclose your real name and title now?"

The companion drew herself up to her full
height and looked down on the old servant
majestically. All the aristocrat — so long con-
cealed beneath a garb of dependence—shone from
her eyes and sounded in her voice as she replied :

"There is no need for you to remind me of
my duty, Matthews. I forgot it once, but I shall
never do so again. Lady Diana Melstrom is dead
—sleeping in her far-off grave under the skies
of Italy. You need not fear that she will ever
come to life again. You know, notwithstanding
the disguise I have assumed, the trouble I have
had to preserve myself from recognition whenever
any of my relations have visited Gardenholme,
and had it not been for Lady Culwarren's coolness
with all our family, and occasional assistance from
you, I hardly know how I should have accomplished

it. Do you think that, after all these years of banishment and shame, I can have any intention of discovering myself now—to receive, perhaps in person, those comments which my sister-in-law was pleased to make concerning me to Mr. Ashfold?"

"She would never have spoken like that, my lady, if she had known you were standing by."

"Perhaps not. Still, I have heard them. My heart may break, Matthews, but my child shall never, through my means, blush for his mother's shame. Let him think of himself as he may. Let him think of his unknown parents as he will. *My* lips shall never fix the stamp of bastardy upon his innocent brow."

"Oh, my lady, will it not be more than your strength can bear?" demanded Matthews, anxiously.

"If so, I can but die, as it would have been better if I had died years ago. No, dear nurse, don't caress me. I want to harden myself—to regard this new fact in the same spirit in which I have learned to regard my living death. Help me to arrange my dress, and put away this tell-tale hair, and then leave me—leave Miss Paget, the companion of the Countess of Culwarren—to wrestle with her heart and resume the character she never again intends to part with."

"And what shall I tell her ladyship, Miss Paget?" asked the old servant, when she had performed the duties required of her.

"Say I am recovered, but feel so weak that, with her permission, I will remain in my room until the evening. And let no one disturb me, Matthews, not even Miss Lily. I wish to be entirely alone."

The old woman crept away to do her bidding, and Miss Paget, advancing to the open window, leaned out of it, to cool her heated face in the soft summer breezes, and try to still the throbbing of her heart. There was a sound of laughter in the air—gay voices and light jests made themselves audible every now and then through the screen of the surrounding foliage, and, by comparison, her sad thoughts grew more sad.

"So used *I* to laugh," she said, to herself,

"and so I jested, until *he* crossed my path, and turned all my mirth to misery."

At length a voice, more ringing and more buoyant than the rest, sounded from the path beneath her window. Miss Paget recognised it in a moment. It was that of Anthony Melstrom speaking to Lilian Osprey. Her first impulse was to gloat, with all the pride of new possession, on his beloved face and figure. But before he had come in view, a horrible shrinking, which was almost fear, overpowered her, and drawing back hastily, she sank down upon the floor and wept without restraint.

"I cannot meet him," she moaned; "I dare not see him. I have not even the courage to look into the face of my own child! Merciful Heaven, have pity upon me. My punishment is greater than I can bear."

CHAPTER X

A BROTHERS' QUARREL.

IT may well be supposed that the desires of Anthony Melstrom did not all tend in the direction of the new conservatory and the billiard-room, when he invited Lord Culwarren and Lilian Osprey to accompany him in a tour of inspection of Gardenholme. He was longing to catch, if it were only one glance, from the eyes of the girl he loved, away from the surveillance of his mother, and he did not consider that the presence of his brother, beside whom they had grown up together and who was so well acquainted with their youthful attachment, would prove any bar to his wishes. The few glimpses he had caught of her face across the luncheon-table had not been very encouraging. Lily had blushed deeply each time their eyes had met, but

she had appeared shy, restless, and strangely ill at
ease before him, and the circumstance had filled
his heart with sad forebodings. The gaiety with
which he had challenged her to a stroll with him
had all been forced. His real object was to find
out how matters stood between them, and if
anything or anybody had come between his heart
and hers during their enforced separation. Lord
Culwarren, on the other hand, was equally anxious
to let his younger brother know that he must give
up all pretensions to their cousin. A few words
which he had exchanged with the Countess before
leaving the luncheon-room made him feel justified
in taking this step, for she had called him to her
side and whispered to him, with a smile and a
pressure of the hand, that all was right, and she
had as good as made the fact of the engagement
patent to their friends. Under these circumstances, it would naturally be supposed that the
newly betrothed lover would have sought the
society of his *fiancée* to thank her for acceding
to his proposal. But something in Lilian Osprey's
manner was more repellent to Culwarren even

than to Anthony. If she was shy and distant with the younger brother, she was positively afraid of the elder, and the Earl felt very much as if he were *de trop* as he sauntered beside the pair.

As soon as they were clear of the luncheon-room and out of sight of the servants, Anthony took Lily's hand and drew it within his arm. At the same moment Culwarren offered his to her. The girl drew back from both.

"No, no!" she said, shaking her head in an agitated manner. "I had better not, thank you. Aunt Emily is so very particular."

"Particular? By Jove! she must be indeed, if she objects to your taking your cousin's arm," exclaimed Anthony, laughing, as he tried to regain possession of her hand. "Nonsense, Lily. I've been without you too long, and refuse to give up any of my privileges now I've returned. One would think you were a young lady introduced to me for the first time."

"At all events, there can be no objection to your taking *my* arm," interposed Culwarren, significantly.

"I would rather not," replied Lily, shrinking away.

Anthony shot one glance of reproach at her, and then addressed his brother.

"Well, Culwarren, so we are once more together. I wonder if you find me as changed as I do you. I don't believe I should have known you in the street. You have cultivated such an indisputable moustache since we parted, and you wear your hair so long. Is that the latest fashion? And how you have been going in for literature, too! I saw your name in red letters a foot high on some placards at the railway station as we came along."

"Yes, yes," replied the Earl in a drawling tone, "it begins to be pretty well known by this time, I believe. You see, Anthony, a man must do *something* nowadays. It has become quite the thing for our class to go in for music, or acting, or writing, and it doesn't do to be behindhand. It used to be only the lower classes that *did* anything, but since the Royal Family have gone in for fiddling, and sculpture, and literature, it is time, of course, that *we* should follow suit."

" Exactly so, as old Ashfold says. But how do you manage it, Culwarren ? Who writes the books for you ? "

The young Earl laughed uneasily and pulled his moustache.

"Oh, come now, Anthony, that's too bad, 'pon my soul. *I* write them, of course. I don't mean to say that everybody could do it; but when you have the *entrée* to good society, it's not so difficult after all. You hear so many stories, you know, and have so many things repeated to you, and the people themselves put ideas into your head. They're such fools, they give themselves away, till it becomes very much like writing from dictation."

" Do you mean to say that you take advantage of your intimacy with certain families to show their secrets up in print ? " demanded young Melstrom, quickly.

" Oh dear, no. I don't put real names, so no one can recognise them except their friends, but that is just what makes the books sell. So many people buy them to see if they know anything of the characters. My last novel, 'Lady Barbara's Secret,' was written on something that Mallett told me about Lady Barbara Ribstone, and by Jove! he made me pay him ten pounds for it, too. And you should have seen how they flew for that book. The libraries had to take twice the usual number. It was an enormous success."

"I am sorry to hear it, Culwarren. I can imagine an author giving a sly cut now and then at his enemies, but I could not have believed it possible that any gentleman would ridicule or expose the follies of those from whom he had received hospitality or kindness. I am afraid, from what you say, that the report I heard last month at Florence must be true."

"What report?"

"That this season several houses have closed their doors to you."

The Earl reddened with displeasure.

"That's all nonsense. It was no such thing. Somebody must have spread the report out of

malice because I didn't patronise him. *Our* class
is always subject to a good deal of envy and
uncharitableness."

"Perhaps. At the same time, we are equally
dependent with what *you* are pleased to term 'the
lower classes' on the goodwill and support of
our acquaintance. I think you will find I have
rubbed off a good many of my aristocratic
prejudices abroad, Culwarren, and it would do
you good to knock about as I have done. It
would teach you to appraise your fellow-creatures
for their worth rather than their birth, and to
value kindness too much ever to dream of abusing
it. What says my little cousin? Lily, I have
hardly heard your voice since I came home. Is
anything the matter, dear? Are you not well?"

"Oh, yes, Anthony, thank you. I am quite
well."

"I can't say you look so," continued Melstrom,
as he scrutinised her features. "You are very
pale, and I'm sure you have been crying. I hope
that is not because you have got your naughty
'Tony' home again."

Lily grew scarlet.

"Oh, no," she ejaculated, timidly.

"Do you know how I have been dreaming of this moment?" he went on, hurriedly; "how I have longed to see Gardenholme again? Had it not been for my mother's embargo, I should have returned long ago. You may be sure of that. But perhaps it was better I should wait till I was free. You have not forgotten that I come of age to-day, Lily?"

"Oh, no," she reiterated, in the same fluttered manner.

"And I intend to enter on my inheritance, too," said the young man, proudly, "whether others object to it or not."

"*Your inheritance!*" repeated the Earl, frowning. "I did not know that you came into any, Anthony."

"*Lily* does," rejoined young Melstrom, gaily. "Lily and I have often talked over my coming of age, and the good things I was to inherit then. There is no necessity for *your* comprehension, Culwarren. Lily and I know all about it."

"I must say you have both religiously kept the secret, then," replied the Earl, very stiffly, "and I think I have the right to——"

"Culwarren," exclaimed the girl, nervously, "had I not better go back to Aunt Emily? She always requires me about three."

"Certainly. By all means," he replied.

"What! going to leave us?" cried Anthony. "That *is* a disappointment. Never mind, though; I will see you later. I *must* see you, darling, and speak to you before the sun goes down."

He smiled lovingly upon her as he spoke, but she dared not return his glance as she ran away in the opposite direction. The brothers entered the new billiard-room in silence. Unconsciously, a great constraint had fallen upon both of them. Anthony took up a cue and sent a ball spinning across the table.

"How Fosbrooke will delight in this," he said; "it is a magnificent table."

"Ah, what about this cosmopolitan friend of yours, Anthony? Who is he, and where did you pick him up? I suppose he is one of those excellent people whom you wish me to value for his worth rather than his birth, eh?"

"His birth is as good as our own," returned Anthony, quickly. "I will vouch for that. As for his *worth*," laughing softly to himself, "poor dear Fosbrooke! He has been thoroughly kind and good to me—the most congenial friend I ever had—but I don't know whether I can say much for his general respectability. I suppose the majority of people would call him a regular scamp, but every word and action betrays he is a gentleman. Yet he is very reticent concerning himself."

"Who are his friends or relations?"

"I have never asked him. His family, I believe, reside in England, but I perceived as soon as we met that he wished his own silence to be respected by his acquaintance."

"Well, I hardly consider you are justified in introducing a man of whom you know so little at Gardenholme. He may be a sharper."

"No, no, Culwarren. I am not quite so simple as you would like to make me. Fosbrooke had the *entrée* to the best houses in Rome, and was hand in glove with all the nobility there. I saw at once that he was a gentleman of birth, education, and manners. He is wild, I grant you—some might call him reckless—and he prefers Bohemian society to the dull respectability of the domestic circle. But at the same time he has a noble and generous heart, is an immense favourite with men, and can ingratiate himself with women as quickly as the most polished courtier in Europe."

"And yet you have never inquired about his antecedents? It is incredible," said the Earl.

"I have alluded to them, but finding he changed the subject, I followed his example. He is a much older man than I am, remember, and treats me with more kindness than familiarity. But I am sure you will like him. No one could help doing so. He has all the fervour of youth joined to the experience of age. Were I not certain of the welcome he will ensure for himself, I should not venture to introduce him to my mother's society. But to speak of other matters, Culwarren," continued Anthony, with an effort, "tell me a little more about yourself. Our correspondence has been so desultory that I am a perfect stranger to your private affairs. Are you completely wedded to the Muses, or have no bright eyes had the power yet to make you feel fickle? You are getting on, you know, old fellow. Twenty-five last birthday. It is high time you were thinking of turning my mother into the Dowager Countess of Culwarren, eh?"

It was with a nervous laugh that Anthony Melstrom finished this peroration and looked up inquiringly into his brother's face. Something in the manner of both the Earl and Lily Osprey had shaken his confidence in himself, and made him anxious to put the question point-blank and learn the truth at once. Culwarren did not know how to answer him. He wanted to say outright that he was engaged to be married to his cousin; but when it came to the point, his mother's assurance was not sufficient for him. He wished now that he had spoken to the girl himself, and been able to make the announcement on their joint authority; but since that was impossible, he made the most of the information that had been afforded him.

" None of the beauties of the season had much effect upon me, Anthony. The best-looking amongst them appeared to me to be an overrated woman."

"But it is not necessary for a girl to be beautiful in order to excite love," replied Anthony. " For my part, I think that brightness and sweetness of expression outweigh the most faultless features."

" Like Lily's, you mean ? " rejoined Culwarren.

"Yes, she is sweet enough, Heaven knows," said Anthony, quickly. " I wonder where I could find her ? I am longing to speak to her for a few minutes alone. You know, Culwarren, perhaps, that my mother—most unjustly, I think—forbid my corresponding with her whilst abroad ? "

" But I don't see why you should have wished to correspond with her," replied his brother. " Miss Paget and my mother were surely able to give you all necessary information respecting her ? "

" Perhaps so ; but it was not sufficient for my happiness. Lily and I have been brought up like brother and sister, and may have been supposed to like interchanging our ideas or memories."

"That's nonsense," interrupted Culwarren, rudely. "As a rule, brothers and sisters don't care a pin for writing to each other, and my mother was quite right in forbidding Lily to waste her time scribbling letters when she had her studies to pursue."

"You cannot deceive me, Culwarren. My mother had but one motive in her prohibition, and that was to separate us altogether."

"If so, she had her own reasons for the act, and knows what is best for the girl."

"What could be better for her than to gain the love and protection of a husband who would always be true to her? My mother might die any day, and you might marry, and in either case Lily cannot remain at Gardenholme."

"She will be married herself before either contingency takes place."

"Perhaps so; but why am not I to try my chance with her as well as others? *You* knew of my attachment to her, Culwarren, before I went abroad, and it has suffered no diminution since. Will you not use your influence with my mother to obtain her permission for me to marry my cousin Lily? My mother loves you far more than she does me. Your word is law with her. Will you exercise it on my behalf? I have returned home with the sole object of marrying Lily Osprey, and if I am baulked of it, I shall go away for ever, for I shall feel I have no home left in England."

"You seem to have been practising elocution over there," replied the Earl, sarcastically; "but I'm afraid it will be lost at Gardenholme. My mother's mind is made up on this subject, and so for the matter of that is Lily's."

"*Lily's!*" cried Anthony. "Has she, then, spoken of it? Has she learnt to regard me with indifference?"

"Her conduct shows plainly enough that she has forgotten all about you."

"What do you mean?"

"That she has another lover."

Anthony Melstrom's fresh face became as pale as ashes.

" Culwarren, is this true? For God's sake do not trifle with me. For the last twelve months I have lived upon the thought that when this day dawned I should be free, in spite of all opposition, to ask Lily to be my wife. In troubles and scrapes of all kinds—when I was laid upon a bed of fever, when I lost friends, or heart, or hope, one idea buoyed me up—that if I lived, the time *must* come when I should be master of my fate and free to woo and marry Lilian Osprey. And when I add, Culwarren, that the same anticipation has had the power to keep me pure and faithful to her, I am sure you will think the higher of an affection that proved such a safeguard to me."

But with each word uttered by his brother, Lord Culwarren's discomposure and confusion increased until he saw no way out of his embarrassment except by roughly telling him the truth.

"It is of no good talking in this way, Anthony," he said, " because the long and the short of it is that the girl doesn't care for you."

" I will not believe it except from her own lips.

Lily may have, as you assert, another lover, but that does not prove that she is false to me."

"Yet she is engaged to be married to him."

At this announcement young Melstrom became much excited.

"Culwarren, why did you allow it? Why did you not warn me of what was impending? You knew my love for her—none better. Why did you not write and inform me there was a rival in my path?"

"Because I consider one man has as good a right to a girl as another, and it would have been altogether against my mother's wishes had I done as you say."

"*Lily engaged*," continued Anthony, incredulously; "I cannot believe it. She seemed so very true. I understand now why she has been afraid to meet my eye since my return. She knows I have the right to accuse her of her perfidy."

"I don't see you have any right at all," replied Culwarren, hastily. "Lily is free to make her own choice in marriage, and my mother will be highly incensed if you presume to mention the subject to her without permission."

"I am a man now, and my mother does not come between me and any woman. Who is this man to whom she has promised my cousin's hand?"

"Do you intend to run him through in the melodramatic style of Italian *inamorati*?" inquired Culwarren, with a sneer.

"Heaven knows. I believe I shall hardly have control of myself if we meet. What is his name?"

"Under the circumstances," replied the Earl, "it would be wiser not to tell you."

Something in his tone made the truth break upon young Melstrom's mind. He stopped short and confronted his brother.

"Culwarren, who is this man? I will know."

"Well, I suppose you can hardly murder him because the girl prefers him to yourself, and so you may as well hear his name to-day as to-morrow. The unworthy individual on whom Miss Lilian Osprey has consented to bestow the honour of her hand happens to be—*myself.*"

As the last words left his lips, the Earl almost started aside from the expression that overspread Anthony Melstrom's face.

"No," said the young man, mournfully, as he observed his action, "there is no need for you to shrink from me, Culwarren. I shall not strike you—not in that way. But," he went on, with clenched teeth and a look of determination, "I will learn the truth of your assertion from Lily's own lips, and if you have lied to me or my mother has coerced her inclination, I will take her from you, were it out of your very arms."

"You cannot do it. She is my betrothed wife."

"Since when?"

"This morning."

"Since you received my letter announcing my return. I see through my mother's finesse and yours. Culwarren, I came home with a heart full of love for you, and in one moment you have changed me into an enemy. Coward! to step between me and the love of my life, as soon as my back was turned and I was unable to plead my own cause. Had you won her from me in fair fight, I could have forgiven you and loved you still, but this is a treacherous act which it will take your life or mine to wipe out again."

"Where are you going?" demanded Lord Culwarren, as Anthony strode away from him.

"Straight into the presence of Lilian Osprey, wherever she may be, to demand an explanation of her conduct."

"But you cannot commit such an outrage. You will probably find her with my mother or surrounded by our friends. This is not the time to enter upon such a subject."

"I care nothing for time or place. You should have considered such things before you made your communication to me. You rob me of the best hope of my life, and expect me to sit down quietly under the intelligence, as though it was the loss of a few hundred pounds."

"But you cannot see Lily now," repeated the Earl, uneasily. All his own hopes seemed vanishing before the impetuosity of his younger brother.

"*Who* is to prevent me?" exclaimed Anthony,

loudly. "Not you nor my mother, nor the whole world! I *will* see her, and hear her story. Until then, I do not kr ɔw whether to treat you as a brother in misfortune, who has fallen in the wiles of an artful coquette, or as a thief who has stolen into my house during my absence and robbed me of the best treasure I possessed."

Saying which, young Melstrom broke away from the detaining clasp which the Earl would have laid upon him, and re-entered the Abbey.

N

CHAPTER XI

OUTCAST ANTHONY.

WHEN Lilian Osprey ran away from the two brothers she was fairly frightened. She was not a cowardly girl by nature, but she was young, and timid, and shy, and had never had a real opportunity to exercise the courage that was in her. She was in the position of an animal that submits to bit and bridle because it does not know its own power, and that it could break away and be free if it chose to do so. She was attached to both her cousins, and she had been brought up to show the strictest obedience to all her aunt's commands. She had no dislike to Culwarren, therefore, but she shrank from the idea of marriage with him, and she dreaded every moment they were together that he would tell Anthony of the half consent that had been wrested from her; and now that she had seen Anthony again, she felt she had been untrue to herself in making such a concession, and that it could never be fulfilled. So she made her escape with a twofold object—the first, to avoid the dangerous glance of her lover's eyes; the second, to find Miss Paget and tell her exactly what she felt upon the subject. It was true that Miss Paget had disclaimed all belief in the truth or purity of love, and that she had warned her that to trust in it was to build her hopes of security upon a lie, and Lily had half believed her. But then Anthony had not returned. Anthony had not looked at her with love and faith beaming in his eyes. Anthony's restored presence had not shown her the state of her own heart, and made a marriage with Culwarren seem impossible. Lily flew from room to room to find Miss Paget and tell her all this. But the companion was not to be found. She had a headache—so some of the servants said—and was asleep in her own room, and the Countess was busily engaged with Mr. Ashfold, and the rest of the company were out walking or in the drawing-room. So the girl went and seated herself in a little retreat, hidden by flowering bushes and luxuriant creepers, which went by the name of the Lady's Bower. As she settled herself upon the rustic bench, her hand moved mechanically to the bosom of her dress, and she drew from it an old stained and faded glove—one which Anthony, in the hurry of departure a twelvemonth since, had thrown upon the floor of his bedroom, and she had picked up and cherished as a keepsake. She looked at it as it lay upon her lap, a soiled and misshapen piece of dogskin, but with the impress of his hand left in it, and a few tears rose to her eyes and fell upon the relic of her youthful love. She was sitting thus, with her moist eyes fixed upon the old glove, when the hanging creepers which formed a door to the Lady's Bower were suddenly pushed aside, and Anthony Melstrom stood before her. Not finding her in the Abbey, he had come by instinct to the spot which had been their favourite place of meeting in the days of old. And when he saw Lily sitting there, with her glorious eyes dimmed by tears, and a soft languorous melancholy in her attitude and appearance, the young man forgot for the moment the question he had come to ask her, and remembered only that they met alone after a whole year's separation, and that she was more beautiful than ever.

" Lily ! " he exclaimed, eagerly ; " my dearest Lily ! I have been longing and praying for this moment.

He clasped her without resistance in his arms, and kissed her on her lips a dozen times, and she was too agitated, and frightened, and delighted, all in one and at the same moment, to be able to think of anything except that Anthony loved her still.

" Tony," she murmured ; " dear, *dear* Tony ! "

" Are you glad to see me, Lily ? "

" Very, *very* glad."

" But there are tears upon your cheek, darling. How came they there ? Not with thoughts of me, I hope ? "

Then Lily remembered, and drew backward.

"Oh, Anthony, you must not stay here with me. Aunt Emily would be so angry. Pray, pray go away. Supposing she were to come and find you here?"

"What of it if she did? Have I not as good a right to speak to you as any other man? I am no longer a child, Lily, to be coerced by my mother's will and frightened at her frown. I have returned to England, prepared to give her all the affection and duty due from a son to his mother; but I am a man now, of an age not only to know my own wishes, but to accomplish them; and those who desire to remain friends with me must learn to acknowledge my right to guide myself."

"Oh, Anthony, you must not talk to me like this. Indeed, I cannot listen to you. Pray let me go. You know Aunt Emily strictly forbid me to—to—think about you any more."

She slid from his embrace as she spoke, and sank down again upon the rustic bench, whilst he regarded her action gloomily and in silence.

"So," he exclaimed, after the lapse of a few seconds that seemed like hours to the conscience-stricken Lily; "so what Lord Culwarren affirms is, I suppose, true, and you are the affianced wife of my elder brother, Lily?"

"Oh, no—that is to say, Aunt Emily spoke to me about it this morning, and I said—— Oh, Tony, do not look at me like that," cried the girl, cowering before him with her face hidden in her hands.

"I want no reasons—no excuses from you. I only want the truth. Have you promised to marry Culwarren or have you not?" asked the young man, sternly.

"I couldn't help it. Aunt Emily made me."

"Have you promised or have you not?" he thundered at her, in a voice which might have been heard half over the grounds of Gardenholme.

"Yes," she answered, faintly; "but—but——"

"And this is the girl who said she *loved* me!" interposed young Melstrom, sarcastically.

"Oh, Tony, I *did* love you. I *do* love you, indeed—indeed I do!" she cried, with bitter tears. "This year of silence and separation has been a year of torture to me. Each day I have thought of you, each night I have prayed for you."

"And you expect me to believe that, when you are engaged to my brother Culwarren. What are you going to marry him for? Have you sold yourself for a coronet and a good rent-roll? Well, then, let him keep his bargain. I wish him joy of it."

"Aunt Emily says I—I—owe everything to her," sobbed Lily, "and I—I—can only repay her thus."

"Pshaw! The case is bad enough as it stands. Don't add to it by a subterfuge. I can quite imagine what Aunt Emily said to you. I am a younger son and a pauper. I am never likely to have either the title or the money, neither am I a literary genius. So Culwarren is in every respect a better match, and I—*I* may go to the d—l."

"Oh, Tony! you are cruel—you do not know."

"I know more than enough, Miss Osprey, in knowing that you will soon be my sister. And I hope after that event happens that I shall never see your face again."

" Let me go! let me go! my heart is breaking," cried Lily, as she ran past him and entered the Abbey. Anthony Melstrom followed her as far as the lawn, which he paced rapidly, with his bitter thoughts reflected on his face.

" Well, well, that dream is over," he said to himself. " It is best that I should know the truth at once, however rudely. Everything seems gone from me now. Mother, brother—and—and—wife! There is no longer any place for me at Gardenholme. I never much cared about the old Abbey. There are few sweet memories of home and childhood in my breast, and those I must make it a duty to forget. I will leave it again as soon as possible, and return to those scenes which have no power to torture me with recollections of the past."

At this moment a servant approached him with a card upon a salver.

" The carriage has returned from Dearham, sir, and the gentleman is waiting to see you."

"Fosbrooke, by Jove!" ejaculated Anthony. "If all this business hasn't put him completely out of my head. Where is Lady Culwarren, James?"

"In the library, sir, with Mr. Ashfold."

"Well, show Mr. Fosbrooke out here, and tell her ladyship of his arrival. Hallo, my dear fellow!" continued Anthony, as Fosbrooke appeared on the lawn, "I'm so glad you've come. I begin to be sick of civilised life already. My mother will be here directly. She is engaged on business with the family lawyer."

"And what were you stamping about the lawn for in that dramatic manner, Anthony?" said Fosbrooke. "I watched you for some minutes from the drawing-room window. What's up? Are you going in for private theatricals, and were you rehearsing to the shrubs and garden benches?"

"My rehearsal was for the acting of a more serious drama than you anticipate, Fosbrooke."

"Not a tragedy, I hope, dear boy?"

"Unlikelier things have happened. Anyway, it's bound to prove a tragedy for me."

" Then there's a woman at the bottom of it ? "

" Why should you say so ? "

" Because, my dear fellow, women have formed the mainspring of all the plots of all the tragedies this world has ever seen. At eighteen we think them angels; at twenty-five they have dwindled into ordinary comforts ; at thirty we pronounce them to be extraordinary nuisances; and I should be afraid to say what name we give them by the time we're forty."

" Were you always such a cynic, Fosbrooke ? "

" Oh dear, no ! I didn't find them out for a long time. I'm only giving you the benefit of my experience. How do you feel about them yourself ? Are you quite disposed to bless the sex at this moment ? "

" Heaven knows I am not," replied Anthony, with a deep sigh.

" That's a real sigh, and I don't like to hear it," said Fosbrooke, seating himself upon a garden roller. " Come, now, Anthony, since it seems I have guessed the cause of your melancholy, let me hear the whole story."

Anthony went up to Fosbrooke and placed his hand affectionately on his shoulder.

"You hold a strange influence over me," he said. "I know no man to whom I can speak as I can to you. I have told you how I loved my cousin Lily, and how much I trusted in her faith to me. I deceived myself, Fosbrooke. It was all a chimera. I returned home eager to claim her for my wife, and I find she is engaged to marry my elder brother."

"Your elder brother? How like a woman!" exclaimed Fosbrooke. "But bear it like a man, old fellow. Such a girl isn't worthy of you."

"I will never give her up," cried young Melstrom, wildly. "You don't know what I feel for her. I will pursue her wherever she may go. I will wrest her from Culwarren's arms at the very altar. I will——"

"Hush, hush, my dear boy," said Fosbrooke, quickly; "you don't want all the world to hear you, surely, and there are ladies coming this way."

And, in effect, there issued from the Abbey at that moment Lady Culwarren with her arm around the neck of Lilian Osprey, followed by Mr. Ashfold and the Earl. Anthony and Fosbrooke rose at their approach.

" This is your friend, Anthony," said the Countess, in her bland tones ; " pray introduce him to us."

"Mr. Fosbrooke—Lady Culwarren, Miss Osprey, Lord Culwarren, Mr. Ashfold," said Anthony, in a constrained voice.

" This is a pleasure, Lady Culwarren, to which I have long looked forward," commenced Fosbrooke. " My young friend and *bon camarade* here—who I regret to see is not in his usual good spirits this morning—has often talked with warmth to me of the various members of his family."

" Very dutiful of him," replied the Countess, coldly.

" Especially of Miss Lilian Osprey, whom I trust I see quite well," continued Fosbrooke, significantly.

" My niece is in perfect health, I thank you."

" I am rejoiced to hear it. Anthony, during

our ramblings together, has often, with the glad confidence of youth, anticipated the happy moment when he should meet again with his mother, his brother, and—*his cousin.*"

"Fosbrooke, pray be silent," pleaded Anthony.

" My dear boy, why should I not allude to an enviable predilection on your part, which is doubtless as patent to others as to myself? Especially to Lady Culwarren.   A mother's eye sees as quickly as heart feels."

The Countess assumed a look of the utmost surprise.

"I am quite in the dark, Mr. Fosbrooke, and have not the least idea to what predilection on the part of Mr. Melstrom you are alluding."

" *No idea!* " cried Anthony, starting forward. " Oh, mother, however painful, let us understand each other.   You must have known of my attachment to my cousin Lily ; I told it you with my own lips. Speak to my mother, Lily," he continued, appealingly, to the girl, who was red and white by turns ; " don't be afraid to tell the truth, and clear me from the accusation of presumption.   Say that whatever may have happened since, we *did* love each other dearly, and exchanged a sacred promise of fidelity. What—you are silent! Are you so false, or I grown so unworthy, that a word is too much now to bestow on him who once possessed your heart?"

"I shall not allow my niece to answer you," said Lady Culwarren, as she wound her arms around the girl's slight figure. "Not a word, Lily, if you please. Remember it is my order."

"You may forbid her to open her mouth, madam," said Anthony, angrily; "but you cannot prevent her heart speaking. As for *you*, Culwarren, I say before every one that you are a traitor. *You* knew well enough that I considered myself engaged to Lilian Osprey, yet you stepped between us and bought her, through my mother's intervention, for the value of a title or so much per annum."

"I will not tolerate this language any longer," cried the Countess. "Be silent, sir, at once, or quit my presence."

"You are my *mother*, madam, and therefore I

will obey you," said Anthony.   "But, *as* my mother, I would appeal to you to——"

"I am *not* your mother!" exclaimed Lady Culwarren, who was too angry to remember what she was saying.   "You are no son of mine."

The little lawyer approached her hastily and plucked her by the sleeve.

"Exactly so.   But let me entreat your ladyship to be cautious.   This is no time or place——"

The Countess turned upon him sharply.

"Have you been telling me the truth or not?"

"The truth, of course, your ladyship."

"Then be good enough to allow me to manage the matter as I will."

During this colloquy Anthony had turned aside, silent and distracted, but as soon as it was concluded he addressed the Countess again.

"In affection, perhaps, you are *not* my mother. Heaven must judge between us; but I know you have never loved me as a son.   Yet, however much we may wish it, we cannot unmake facts, and the fact remains that I am your own child."

"It is *not* a fact," cried Lady Culwarren,

shrilly; "it is a falsehood. I have but *one* child, and this is he." And as she spoke she laid her hand upon the shoulder of the Earl.

"You renounce me, then?" said Anthony, in a voice of pain.

"You are not mine to renounce," replied the Countess. "I tell you again—I tell all the world —that you are not my son."

A dead pause followed this extraordinary announcement. The assembled guests looked at their hostess and the handsome young man who had so lately joined them in amazement, and a sudden premonition of approaching trouble seemed to strike all present. Anthony Melstrom passed his hand in a dazed manner across his brow, and his friend Fosbrooke drew nearer to him and laid his hand upon his arm. Melstrom shook it off, as though daring the world to say he could not stand alone. In a little while he spoke again.

"Not your son?" he reiterated. "*Who* am I, then?"

Lady Culwarren's eyes shone with malicious triumph as she replied:

"You are a man without a name—a man whose mother's name is stained with shame—a bastard substitute for my dead child."

"It's a lie!" cried Anthony, fiercely; "a black and bitter lie. I don't believe it."

"Mr. Ashfold," said the Countess, coldly, "the leading documents which prove this *lie* are in your possession. Perhaps you will be good enough to show them to this young gentleman, and convince him of the accuracy of my statement. He can hardly be expected to believe it otherwise."

"Exactly so," said the solicitor. "I regret the time and place that have been chosen for imparting so delicate and unfortunate a piece of news, but the late Earl's papers leave no room for its denial. I shall be happy to show them to you, Mr. Melstrom, if you will accompany me to the library."

But Anthony seemed to have heard nothing but the fatal news. He staggered back towards Fosbrooke, murmuring:

"For God's sake tell me, is this some fearful dream?"

"I think it is time we ended this painful interview, which Mr. Melstrom brought entirely on himself," remarked Lady Culwarren, as she turned to re-enter the Abbey. But Lily's forbearance had reached its utmost limit. She broke from her aunt's encircling clasp, and rushing back to Anthony, threw herself into his arms, exclaiming:

"Oh, Anthony, dear Anthony! If all others forsake you, I will be true. Try me, Anthony! Take me with you. I cannot remain here alone. Oh, Anthony, I love you—I love you!"

But Anthony put her forcibly away.

"Don't touch me," he said, in a voice of horror; "don't speak to me. Remember what I am!"

"No, no! I remember nothing but that you are my first, my only love. Tony, I have never forgotten you. I was persuaded into renouncing you. I am yours, and yours only."

He placed his hand upon her head, and raised it so that he could look into her eyes.

"Yes," he ejaculated, "you have told me the

truth. Poor child, you love me still. But your protestations come too late. No power on earth could make me now link my outcast fate with yours."

"Nor should I permit it, as guardian of my niece," interposed Lady Culwarren, as she drew Lily away. "I forgive you, my dear, because you evidently don't know what you are doing; but I cannot allow you to expose yourself in this terrible manner any longer. As for you, Mr. Melstrom, you will quit the Abbey, if you please, and return to it no more. Miss Osprey shall not be subjected to your attentions again."

"You will not find me slow to obey you, madam. The recollection of these walls will become as hateful to me as they were once dear. I shall have no home now but the wide world."

"Tony—Tony, speak to me!" wailed Lily.

"Be happy, darling, if you can, and think of me as little as you may. Come, Fosbrooke, you have encountered a sorry welcome to Garden-holme; but I must leave it, and I know you will stand by me to the end."

"With all my heart, dear boy. It will be a sorry day that sees us estranged. If all the world forsake you, Anthony, you will still find a friend in me. We have been happy enough in our Bohemian life together. Let us return to it and see if it cannot provide sufficient bolts to bar the door effectually against dull care. Nameless, friendless, penniless, what matter? So am I. The inhabitants of the fair land of Bohemia accord the heartiest welcome to those who have been driven out and turn no lingering glances on the false paradise they leave behind them. Come, Anthony, you shall be *my* son."

"One moment, gentlemen," interposed Mr. Ashfold, as they prepared to turn away. "Mr. Melstrom is not quite so penniless as you suppose. The late Earl did not neglect to make arrangements for his maintenance, and I shall be glad to know before we part when and where I can see him to settle the business between us."

"My father," commenced Anthony, and then checking himself with a sob—"I mean Lord Culwarren—was always only too good to me. I shall be at Dearham, Mr. Ashfold, until to-morrow. Perhaps you will wait upon me there and tell me all you know about this miserable business."

He threw one last glance of farewell at the old Abbey, mantled in green, which was brightened by the setting sun, as he spoke. At her bedroom window he encountered the face of Miss Paget, pale and immovable as that of a statue, but staring at him and his companion with eyes of fire. Anthony doffed his felt hat and waved it towards her in farewell.

"Good-bye," he cried aloud, with a reckless laugh. "Good-bye to you and Gardenholme for ever."

And then he clapped Fosbrooke cheerily on the shoulder, and the two men went forth arm-in-arm.

CHAPTER XII.

A SORRY TRIUMPH.

AS they disappeared, an ominous silence fell on the group they left behind them. The guests of Gardenholme did not dare to express their opinions on the matter, but their faces told them plainly enough. Lord Culwarren looked moody and dissatisfied. Lily's head drooped lower and lower to the ground. The solicitor was stroking his chin and meditating. The Countess began to feel uncomfortable and as if she had made a mistake.

"Are they really gone?" she inquired, presently, finding that no one made a remark.

"It looks like it. They are certainly out of sight," replied Ashfold, gazing after them in a melancholy manner.

"But they can't go without the carriage.

Dearham is five miles off. And Mr. Fosbrooke brought the luggage with him. Aren't they going to take it back again? What can they be thinking of?"

"Exactly so. But your ladyship will pardon me for observing that your announcement of this very delicate and painful piece of information was so abrupt that it left them no time for thinking at all."

"Of course not. Nor any one else either," said the Earl; "or I might have been tempted to remind you, mother, before you turned my brother out of Gardenholme, that the Abbey belongs *to me*."

If her son had turned and struck her in the face, he could hardly have given the Countess a greater shock than these words conveyed. It was true that Gardenholme belonged exclusively to him, and that her dower house lay at some distance from it. But she had been accustomed, since his father's death, to order everything about the Abbey, just as she had done in the old days, until she had almost forgotten it had passed out of her possession. And then to be reminded of it before her company and on such an occasion. It made the Countess feel that she had gained her victory too dearly.

"He is not your brother, Culwarren," she answered, in a most subdued manner; "but we will not discuss the question any further now. Lily, my dear, don't hang so heavily on my arm. Take your cousin back to the house, Culwarren. These unpleasant proceedings have quite upset the dear child."

"I should think they were enough to upset any one," replied his lordship, gloomily, as he offered his arm to Lilian Osprey. As he disappeared, Lady Culwarren looked round upon her guests with a sickly smile.

"I'm afraid I owe you all an apology for having made you witnesses to such a painful scene; but it was a duty I owed to myself. The young man has been behaving very badly, and presuming on his supposed relationship to me. Perhaps I should have kept the secret a little longer, but he provoked me to disclose it by his absurd pretensions to the hand of my niece, Miss Osprey, who is already engaged to be married to Lord Culwarren. But it is just as well it is over, and I trust you will all forget it as soon as possible. Mr. Ashfold, will you kindly give me your arm back to the house? The excitement has made me feel quite ill. How annoying it is," she continued, as they moved away, "that Miss Paget should be laid up at this juncture, when she would have been invaluable to me in satisfying the idle curiosity of these people and keeping them amused. What is the matter with you, Culwarren?" she said, as they reached the library, and saw the Earl looking unusually sulky or perplexed. "Do you intend to give me the same trouble as this boy whom your father foisted on me as a son? I consider I have been most cruelly and unjustifiably treated."

"And I consider Anthony might say the same. He has been brought up amongst us from his very birth, without a hint of his not being of the same parentage, and then, without the slightest warning, the truth, accompanied by

the bitterest insult, is flung in his face, and he is
turned out of Gardenholme like a thief or a dis-
charged servant. And *I* stood by and saw it
done."

"Upon my word, you are grateful, Lord
Culwarren," exclaimed the Countess, sarcastically. "Here have I seized upon the opportunity to remove a most dangerous rival from
your path, and all the thanks I receive in return
are to hear my conduct censured by the one I
strove to benefit. You don't seem to understand
what an obstacle to your marriage with Lilian
Osprey lay in the presence of Anthony Melstrom."

"I do understand it perfectly. We nearly came
to blows about it this afternoon, and the girl made
her feelings for him palpable enough just now.
Instead of gaining by your stratagem, mother, I
am far more likely to lose. You have been unjust
to Anthony in Lily's estimation, and I know
enough of women to be aware that they always
sympathise with the injured party. But put that
aside, as I have done, for this business has pretty
well knocked all thoughts of love and marriage

out of my head. The fact remains that you have turned the man who was brought up as your son and my brother out of my house in the most cruel and inhospitable manner, in the presence of your guests, and I must make amends for your behaviour if I can. Mr. Ashfold, are you in my brother's confidence ? Where has he gone ? "

"Mr. Melstrom told me he should be at the 'Culwarren Arms' until to-morrow, my lord."

The Earl rang the bell and ordered the servant to have a carriage at the door as soon as it could be made ready.

" Culwarren, where are you going ? " demanded the Countess, anxiously.

" I am going to Dearham to apologise to the two gentlemen you have treated so discourteously, and to ask Anthony to forgive me for the words that passed between us this afternoon."

"You will humiliate yourself and me," cried his mother, indignantly.

" It will be a noble action, my lord. Exactly so," exclaimed the little lawyer, " and may I ask to go with you ? "

"No, Mr. Ashfold, I would rather go alone," replied the Earl. But a few hours later he returned home crestfallen.

"Anthony refuses to see me," he said, mournfully. "He declines, now or ever, to hold any further intercourse with the house of Culwarren."

"I knew the sort of reception you would encounter," exclaimed the Countess, triumphantly. "This young man, like all low-bred people, can only show his annoyance by insulting his superiors. Anybody could see he had not been born to the position he held here. I suppose his mother was a housemaid. But I have little doubt that he will not scruple to avail himself of the provision made for him by his patron, the late Earl. The whole transaction is the most scandalous thing I ever heard of. It drives me wild even to think of it."

The next day, however, Lady Culwarren's predictions proved to be untrue.

"Mr. Melstrom refuses to accept the three hundred a year unconditionally settled upon him by the late Earl," said Mr. Ashfold, entering the library, after a visit to Dearham. "He declares that his lordship must have done so believing that he would remain as a loved and loving son at Gardenholme, and not be kicked out as a usurper. It is very foolish of him—foolish and quixotic— and so I told him plainly, but I could not alter his resolve. It is his, however, and so there it must remain until he chooses to take it. But this affair has cut him up terribly — terribly — no doubt of that, and his pride is all up in arms. Exactly so."

"Did you ask him to see me? Did you tell him with what purpose I visited Dearham last night?" demanded Culwarren, anxiously.

"I did, my lord, and Mr. Melstrom desired me to thank you for your good intentions, but to say that, under the circumstances, it was better that you should not meet."

"He *shall* see me," exclaimed the Earl, impetuously. "I will ride over there this afternoon."

"It would be useless, my lord. They are gone."

"*Gone!* Where?"

"That I cannot tell you, and I don't think they

knew themselves. But they started as I came away. I shook hands with them as they got into the carriage, and I don't think they are likely to send their address to Gardenholme. Exactly so."

"I would have given everything that I possess that this should not have happened," cried Culwarren, remorsefully, as he hurried from the room.

Everything appeared to grow very stale, flat, and unprofitable at the Abbey after that. The company dispersed as if by magic. Miss Paget, who had come downstairs again, was so pale, and silent, and depressed, and moved about the house so like a ghost, that it inspired melancholy only to look at her. Lily Osprey had become the shadow of her former self. Lord Culwarren seemed to take interest in nothing, and the Countess was always in a bad temper. With the departure of Anthony Melstrom, a cloud had fallen upon Gardenholme, and the old Abbey was speedily given up to its lawful possessors.

"What is the matter with you all?" exclaimed

the Countess, fretfully, some weeks after these
events had happened. " There seems a spell upon
the place. I never knew the house so dull before.
I hear no music nor singing, and no one ever seems
to call. One would think there was a death in the
family. Why don't you do something to enliven
us, Culwarren ? "

"I am not lively enough myself for that,
mother."

"I don't know why you shouldn't be. Where
is Lily ? "

" In her own room, I suppose. I have not seen
her since breakfast-time."

"You should invite her to walk or ride with
you. You have become a laggard in love,
Culwarren. Have you relinquished your desire to
marry your cousin ? "

" By no means, if she will marry me. But I
doubt it. You heard what she said to Anthony
the day he left us. She called him her first and
only love, and declared she was his and his
only. They were not pleasant words for me to
hear, mother, and I have not forgotten them. Nor

is it likely, if they were true, that she will consent to become my wife."

"Oh, that's nonsense! She *has* consented. She told me distinctly that she would do as I pleased in the matter. And as for any foolish ideas she may have given vent to in the excitement of the occasion you mention, you mustn't think any more about it. The girl was hysterical. She has probably forgotten what she did say. It was just on the impulse of the moment. Nothing more."

"The impulse may return when she meets Anthony again."

"She will *never* meet him again," replied the Countess, angrily. "I will renounce any one who keeps up any communication with that young man. I utterly forbid his name being mentioned in my presence."

"Well, well! perhaps it is best so. And when Lily is ready to marry me, mother, I shall be ready to marry her; but not before."

Upon this Lady Culwarren took an early opportunity to sound her niece's wishes on the subject.

"My dear girl does not forget the promise she once gave me to become my daughter," she said, in a loving voice one day, as she passed her jewelled fingers through Lily's hair.

"No, Aunt Emily," replied Lily, trembling.

"Our dear Culwarren is getting rather impatient, love. We are nearly through September, and I should like to see the wedding take place before Christmas. What does my bird say to six weeks hence—the first week in November?"

"Oh, no, aunt, not so soon as that, I beg. It is so sudden. We have never thought of it. Why cannot we remain as we are? We are very happy, are we not?" pleaded the girl, in faltering tones.

Lady Culwarren almost pushed her from her.

"I am tired of all this," she said, petulantly. "You are still hankering after that worthless youth who has passed out of your life altogether. Now, mark my words, Lily! If there were not another man in the world, you should never marry Anthony Melstrom. He is idle, and dissipated, and ungrateful. He cares only for low society, and is probably entitled to no better. He has not even a name to offer you, and if he had, you should never, with my consent, accept it. So put him out of your head at once, and make up your mind to do your duty."

"I will, Aunt Emily—indeed I will. I am trying day and night to do it, only it is so very, *very* hard. But don't ask me to marry any one else—not just yet, for it would break my heart," cried Lily, sobbing.

"Oh, there! Go away, do, Lily, and cry somewhere else, for I am positively sick of all this affectation," said the Countess, impatiently, and she sought her companion with a view of taking counsel of her.

"What *am* I to do with these children, Miss Paget?" she exclaimed; "they seem to me to be positively bewitched. Culwarren has become as indifferent about his engagement to Lily as he was once eager to compass it. And as for the girl, she makes every objection to the proposal that she can, and has really cried so much lately as to actually disfigure herself, which perhaps accounts for her cousin's coolness."

Miss Paget's eyes grew softer than usual, as she listened to this narrative.

"Poor children!" she said; "you must not forget that they have suffered a great shock."

"About Anthony? Well, if it was a shock to them, I am sure it was so to me. I couldn't sleep for nights after. To think that for twenty-one years I had been cherishing some other woman's base-born child in my bosom! I felt as if I had been contaminated."

"Don't regret it, Lady Culwarren," said the companion, earnestly. "Think how the unhappy mother, who for all these years has never known her son, would bless you for any kindness you have shown to him. And I don't believe *he* is ungrateful. He may be wild and thoughtless, and the failure of Lily's love was very hard for him to bear; but he has a warm and generous heart, and he will be the first to regret any hasty words or actions of which he may have been guilty."

"Ah, you always were his advocate from the time he was a little child, Miss Paget. However, though I can't agree with you, as we are never likely to be brought in contact with him again, let us drop the subject. But what should you advise me to do with regard to Lily and Culwarren?"

"Suppose you take them away for a while."

"Leave Gardenholme?"

"Yes. Why not? You have so little change, and every tree and flower here seems fraught now with a sad memory. How can the children help mourning when they remember they are separated, perhaps for ever, from the companion of their youth? Would not a little foreign travel be good for all of you? It would instil fresh ideas in Culwarren's mind, and help Lily to shake off her regretful thoughts, and, by throwing them much together, perhaps bring about the very consummation you so ardently desire."

"Miss Paget, you are a genius! You always hit upon the right thing to do. We will certainly winter abroad. I shall enjoy the change as much as any one, for I am catching the infection of the general dulness, and wish sometimes—well, it's no use saying it now—but I *do* wish sometimes that my husband, having kept his secret for so many years, had kept it to himself for ever."

The companion did not venture to make any comment on the Countess's remark, but she caught her hand and kissed it fervently.

CHAPTER XIII.

IN THE TOILS.

I T was a glorious morning, about the middle of October, in Florence. The soft, balmy air, filled with the odour of the Tuscan violets that bloom above poor Keats's untimely grave, exhilarated the inhaler like a draught of champagne. The sky was an expanse of cloudless blue. In the streets of the city, and on the bridges of the Arno, the flower girls offered their rich bouquets of tuberoses and orange blossoms and heliotrope with lavish generosity, filling the hands of the passers-by for a few scudi, and causing the English visitors to fill the air with their exclamations of surprise and delight. At a little distance from the traffic came a young man walking—almost bounding—from the railway station. He was but a stripling, but he appeared to have all the gay *insouciance* of a child as he pursued his way. He carried his soft felt hat in his hand, and his handsome face, flushed with the rapidity of his motion, was raised to the fair Italian sky. Mirth was on his lips and in his eye as he hurried along the road with some glad anticipation before him. He had just entered some public gardens, which led by a short cut to his temporary home, when a voice from a side path arrested his footsteps. He turned quickly, and saw Oliver Fosbrooke stretched at full length on a garden seat, with his hat tilted over his eyes and a cigar between his lips.

"Hullo, Anthony!" he exclaimed, in a cordial voice. "Back already? I didn't expect you till the next train. It's a sight for sore eyes to see your beaming face, my boy. It seems a week since you left Florence."

"What, can't you do without me for a single day?" said Anthony Melstrom, as he laid his hand affectionately on the speaker's shoulder.

"Not very well, my son. We had a dull evening last night, and I missed your bright face and ready hand every minute. But have you got the money?"

"No fear, Fosbrooke," cried the young man with a laugh. "I frightened him into compliance. I manipulated the name of his mother so deftly that Monsieur le Vicomte fancied I was in communication with her, and shelled out like a bird. Four thousand eight hundred francs, and I took care to cash his note of hand before I accepted it. I have it safe in my belt."

"You're invaluable to me, Tony. Simply invaluable!" said Fosbrooke, with a sigh of relief. "This will enable us to carry on the war gallantly."

"Yes," replied Melstrom, "it's not a job I much care about, Fosbrooke; but in this instance the Vicomte is rich and can well afford to part with it, added to which he is a braggart, and deserves a lesson. If I had not started for Villagio yesterday, I don't think I should have caught him, for his portmanteaux were packed and already addressed to Paris."

"It has been a lucky stroke of business," mused Fosbrooke; "but I *have* been lucky ever since I met you, Tony. Our *rencontre* seems to have been the turning-point of my existence. I shall never forget you saved my life, my boy. I shall never forget that night when I stood before the glass with my revolver in my hand and you knocked at my bedroom door. What a plucky young fellow I thought you then, and how my heart, such as it is, went forth to you, and made me listen to reason administered through the mouth of a suckling! I loved you for it, Tony, and I have loved you ever since."

Anthony sat down on the bench beside his friend as though prepared to enter on a conversation with him.

"When I watched you come bounding along the Villiegatura Road just now, with a glad smile upon your face, I thought how different it looked from what it did two months ago, when we left Gardenholme together, and I hoped it was the happier life you have led with me that wrought the change. You *are* happier, are you not, Melstrom, and have ceased to worry yourself about that which is inevitable?"

Some of the sunshine faded from Anthony's face as he replied:

"Yes, Fosbrooke, I *am* happier; there is no doubt of that. The free life we lead together, the gaieties we pursue, the pleasant company we cultivate, are all conducive to drive care away. Besides, what is the use of caring? I cannot undo the wrong that others have done me. Ashfold's proofs of my stained birth were irrefragable, and I suppose it is scarcely to be wondered at that Lady Culwarren was almost as sore as I was at the discovery. And then I try to convince myself that if Lily had been faithful to me it would have been of no avail. I think she *does* love me, poor child, but she will soon get over it, and I could never have been so base as to persuade her to share my fortunes. If she doesn't exactly *love* Lord Culwarren she *likes* him, and I fancy that few women's attachments go any further. But it is *he* whom I cannot find it in my heart to forgive—the traitor."

"Ah! you cannot forgive *him*," remarked Fosbrooke, thoughtfully; "I'm not surprised at it. Well, some day, perhaps, you may have an opportunity for revenge."

"When I do, I shall take it," replied the youth, flushing.

"It may come sooner than you imagine. Count Biron lost heavily again last night, and so did Captain Tomkins."

"Did they?" remarked Anthony, absently.

"Yes, and I was introduced to two new fellows just arrived in Florence, brothers of the name of Dacre, but I am not sure if they have more than enough of the ready to pay their way."

"Fosbrooke," said Anthony, presently, "there is only one thing I don't care for in this life of ours."

"And what is that, my boy?"

"The high play. It is very amusing and very exciting, but it's what it leads to, Fosbrooke. These men, especially the foreigners, are seldom strictly honourable. I have seen some dirty work since we have been together that I have been afraid to mention lest I should have a stiletto in my heart."

" You're right, my boy. It's a case of diamond cut diamond, but that's the excitement of it. Who cares for a game of neither skill nor chance, and with no reward at the end? Besides, Tony, I don't quite see how you and I would get on without an occasional haul. You have no money, or you don't choose to take it, and I have very little. If we did not live like freebooters on society, I'm afraid we should soon cease to live at all."

"But all our good fortune must come at the expense of others," said the young man, sadly.

" True, dear fellow; but we run an equal chance of loss. If we are quicker or cleverer than the herd, we deserve to win. Besides, they play of their own free will, no one can compel them, and if they are such fools as to go on in the face of ill-luck, it's their look-out and not ours. What, conscience-stricken still, Tony? *I* have no such fine-drawn scruples. I know of a fat pigeon in Florence to-day whom I should dearly love to pluck till he hadn't a feather left upon his carcase."

"Who is that? Prince Ptolemy of Sturin?" asked Anthony, indifferently.

"Prince Ptolemy of Sturin," repeated Fosbrooke, contemptuously. "Some one who carries more money in his pocket, Anthony, than Ptolemy has in the bank. Some one also who might afford *you* the revenge you covet."

"*Culwarren*," cried the young man, starting violently. "Is he in Florence? Have you seen him? Are you sure?"

"One question at a time, *mon cher*. Yes, it is true. The Earl of Culwarren is in Florence, at the 'Hôtel Villa Pomona,' with Lady Culwarren and suite. I saw it in the papers, and I inquired personally last night. There is no doubt about the matter."

"He is married, then," said Anthony, turning deathly pale.

"Probably; it sounds like a wedding trip, doesn't it? But what does that signify to you? It will be all the greater triumph to draw him into the net and drain him dry. I don't see why he should have the girl and her fortune too—do you?"

"By Heaven, no!" exclaimed Anthony, as he rose and paced the garden path. "Get hold of him, Fosbrooke," he continued, with clenched teeth; "grip him, ruin him. If I must suffer, let him suffer too."

"That's right, *mon cher*. *That* shows the stuff that is in you, and is worth ten thousand maudlin thoughts of love. But be advised by me, Tony. Don't go near the 'Hôtel Villa Pomona.'"

"Is it likely? Why should I go there? What is left for me now *she* is gone?"

"There you go again. You cannot see through the folly of that process of imagination which men call love."

"I know you have no faith in its existence, Fosbrooke."

"Pardon me, dear chum. I believe it exists, under certain circumstances, but I know that it never endures. A boy imagines that the possession of the object he longs for will secure the happiness it seems to promise. A man has ascertained that the realisation of desire is not half so sweet as the desire itself."

"You cannot persuade me of that, Fosbrooke. My love is lost to me, and all my hopes are shattered. But there must have been truth in both of them, for neither will ever be succeeded or restored."

Oliver Fosbrooke laughed heartily.

"Forgive me, Tony. You have every right to be angry, but I can't help it," he said. "I know you don't believe me. You never will until you have bought experience for yourself; perhaps as bitterly as I have done. Who, surmising in the summer-tide of life, looks around to the winter storms that toss him to the sea that lies beyond the quiet stream? Who, in the full flush of health, can realise the tortures of disease? Yet there are rocks in the river-bed, my son, storms in the cloudless summer air, cancers lurking beneath apparent health, and misery in love. You are but one-and-twenty, and yet you are experiencing its torture. You will not be really happy until you have learnt to despise its existence."

"Perhaps so, Fosbrooke. But it is a sad religion. However, you need not be afraid that

I shall leave my card upon Lord and Lady
Culwarren. But how will you get hold of him?"

"As easily as possible. I understand that he
feels rather strange in Florence, and hardly knows
what to do with himself. I will throw myself in
his way, and ask him to sup with us at Galanti's.
Then I will offer to be his cicerone through the
city, and the result will be to land him in the
society of our friends. Then for the plucking!
Upon my word, my fingers itch to begin."

"But he will see *me*," said Anthony.

"What matter? Your only cause of difference
was the young lady, and now that he's got her, he
will forget everything that passed between you,
and probably be eager to be friends again. Don't
you remember that he came after you to Dearham,
but you refused to see him? It will be right
enough with his lordship, you may depend upon
that, and if you can put your pride so far in your
pocket as to appear to forgive him, there will be
no difficulty about the matter. By Jove! Tony,
there he comes along that path by the lake, with a
green book in his hand—Swinburne's poems, I'll

be bound—and a cigarette in his mouth. Doesn't he look like a girl dressed up in men's clothes, with his long hair and his rose in his button-hole? Upon my word, he's the greatest sawny I ever met, and Miss Osprey is the young lady with the worst taste I ever knew. I wish her joy of him."

"Fosbrooke, what shall I do?" exclaimed Anthony.

"Stay and meet him, my boy, and be as amiable as you can. Why shouldn't you? You've done no harm."

"But if he should speak to me of her?"

"Don't allow him. Say you decline to discuss the subject. And think of your revenge, my boy! Think of your revenge! We'll make it as glorious as it shall be complete."

Anthony Melstrom, with a fast-beating heart, turned to one side as Lord Culwarren, his eyes bent upon his book, walked leisurely past the bench on which reclined the form of Oliver Fosbrooke.

"Good morning, my lord," he said in his rich, round voice. "This is an unexpected meeting."

The Earl looked up, and the pleasure of the recognition was visible in his face. He advanced rapidly with extended hand.

"Mr. Fosbrooke! Is it possible? This is the last place in the world in which I should have expected to meet you. And is Anthony with you? Is he in Florence?"

"Anthony is here," replied Fosbrooke as he waved his hand towards his young friend. "We have never separated, my lord, since you saw us last, and I trust we never shall."

"Anthony, won't you speak to me?" said the Earl, as he turned to the man he had for so long believed to be his brother.

"If your lordship wishes it," replied Anthony, coldly.

"Your lordship! Has it come to that between you and me, who were always 'Cul' and 'Tony' to each other?" cried Culwarren. "Oh, Anthony, this terrible *exposé* was not of my doing. Had my father's documents been brought to me instead of to my mother——"

"You would doubtless have done your duty

as the Countess did. Pray don't mention it again.
My lot is fixed and I am content with it, and
under the circumstances I can only be grateful
for the many years of hospitality I enjoyed at
your hands and those of your late father's."

"You talk to me as if we were strangers,
Anthony. Why should this unfortunate disclosure
make such a difference between us?"

"I am not aware that it has."

"Yet you are altered. Your manner savours
of offence."

"If so, it has nothing to do with the subject
you mention."

"Then you will let us be friends again, as we
were in the old days before this trouble came
upon us. If I could only make you understand
how disgusted I was at my mother's treatment of
you. It was harsh and unwomanly in the extreme.
Both Lily and I——"

"Stop, Culwarren!" exclaimed Anthony, inter-
rupting him. "You have expressed a wish to be
on friendly terms with me again. It can only be
on one condition—that you never mention that

lady's name in my hearing, nor endeavour to
bring about a meeting between us. Let the dead
past bury its dead. We fought together, and you
are victor. Be generous enough to leave the
vanquished in peace."

"If you wish it, it shall be so," replied Lord
Culwarren; "but I shall not dare, in that case, to
tell her that I have seen you. She is here, of
course, but it is hardly likely you will meet her
without an appointment."

"It is far better you should keep your
own counsel, my lord," interposed Fosbrooke.
"Florence is a charming city, but her best
amusements are those in which ladies cannot
join. If you want to see life, you must leave
your femininities at home."

"I *do* want to see it," exclaimed the young
Earl, eagerly; "I came abroad on purpose to see
a little of the world. Anthony said it would do
me good to mix in Bohemian society, but I've
been cooped up so long at Gardenholme I don't
know how to set about it. I had read so much
of Florence, I was full of anticipations on coming

here.   But it doesn't seem much gayer to me
than other cities, and really on the whole I've been
rather dull."

"Your lordship doesn't know the right way to
go to work," said Fosbrooke.   "It requires a
knowledge of Continental life to get the *entrée* to
the best places of amusement.   Let me and
Anthony be your ciceroni—that is, if you will
not be bound to account for your absence from
the ' Hôtel Villa Pomona.' "

"*Bound!*   No such thing.   Do you suppose
I'm not free to come and go as I choose, Mr.
Fosbrooke?   Besides, I'm engaged on an Italian
romance at the present, and it's absolutely necessary
I should see a few phases of the national life.   I
shall be delighted to join your party.   What time
shall I be with you, and where do you hang out ? "

" I am afraid the quarters which I and Anthony
occupy would rather shock your insular prejudices,
my lord.   What would you say to a huge barrack
of a room at the very top of an old Florentine
Palazzo once owned by the Prince of Salacci, two
beds, a table, and a couple of chairs ; that's about

the amount of our furniture, isn't it, Tony? But
we sleep the sleep of the just all the same, and
are none the worse for the emptiness of our
apartment."

"But how do you manage about your meals?"
inquired Culwarren, curiously.

"We breakfast out of doors, dine out of doors,
sup out of doors, smoke out of doors, and might
sleep out if we felt so inclined, my lord. We live
the life of the birds of the air, are as free, as careless, as easily satisfied, and almost as happy. We are
true Bohemians, Lord Culwarren, and if you would
see something of our existence you must be
prepared to meet our friends."

"There is nothing that would please me better,
Mr. Fosbrooke. I have been longing for a little
excitement. I am sure you must lead a charming
life, and full of pleasure."

"Yes. We have our simple and inexpensive
pleasures," replied Fosbrooke; "a cup of coffee and
a cigarette, a seat at the play, a game at cards or
dominoes. These make up about the sum of our
dissipations."

"How glad I am I came across you!" exclaimed Lord Culwarren, with a beaming face. "Florence will look a different place to me now."

"Will your lordship give us the honour of your company to supper at Galanti's to-night?" continued Fosbrooke. "Doubtless you know the place—at the corner of the Strada Reale. An unpretending little restaurant, but a first-rate *chef*, and a favourite haunt of ours. Will you come?"

"With the greatest of pleasure," replied Culwarren, shaking Fosbrooke's hand. "I must go now, because Lady Culwarren will be expecting me, but I will be sure to be punctual. At what time?"

"Ten o'clock, if that will suit your lordship," and then the men bade each other farewell and separated.

"Lady Culwarren will be expecting him!" repeated Anthony, grinding his teeth. "By Heaven! If he goes on talking like that, I shan't be able to keep my hands off him."

"Softly, softly, *mon cher*," said Fosbrooke; "remember this is your revenge!"

"Yes, and by George it shall be a deadly one! I'll get Braganza or Tomkins or some of those fellows to lead him on until he shoots himself."

"Not quite so far as that, dear boy. You might be tempted to go in for the widow."

"Hush, Fosbrooke! don't jest on that subject. Remember I am *no one*."

CHAPTER XIV.

AN UNPLEASANT DISCLOSURE.

THE pleasant suite of rooms in the "Hôtel Villa Pomona" which had been engaged for the Earl of Culwarren's party was lighted up by the morning sun. Through the open windows came the breath of a thousand flowers. Beneath the casement lay a parterre of orange and citron trees, intermingled with bushes weighed to the ground with their burden of roses and myrtle blossom. Beyond might be seen the deep blue waters of the River Arno, placid as a lake in summer. Breakfast was laid upon the table, and Lady Culwarren, attired in a flowing *peignoir* of muslin, was fanning herself violently at one end of it, whilst Lily Osprey and Miss Paget sat at the other.

"Really, this is all very delightful," exclaimed

the Countess; "fancy our being in November with
such a scene before us! I suppose they are half-
way up to their knees in mud in England by this
time. If I had known that life abroad was half so
charming, I should have visited the Continent
yearly. What do *you* say, Miss Paget?"

The companion was not looking so well as she
had done at Gardenholme. There was a strained
expression about her features that had not been
there before. She looked hopeless, perhaps, but
more anxious; but she smiled cheerfully as she
replied:

"I am quite of your opinion, Lady Culwarren; Florence is like a beautiful dream to
me. I feel as if I could never tire of its ex-
ceeding loveliness."

"And the style of living is so novel and so
much pleasanter than in England. Those Cascine
Gardens, where you can walk about in the evenings
as freely as if you were in your own house. It is
quite entrancing. I shall go there whenever we are
not otherwise engaged. But where is Culwarren?
He is getting very late in the mornings. I wish

he would learn to be a little more punctual. Lily, my love, do ring the bell for François."

But on François being sent to summon the tardy Earl, he returned with the intelligence that milord had not been home all night. Lady Culwarren's face reddened with anger as she heard it.

"The second time this week!" she exclaimed, as soon as the servant had disappeared; "it is too bad of Culwarren. I will not stand it any longer. What can he possibly find to do that should keep him away from us for so many hours?"

"Doubtless he has made acquaintances in the city, and is staying the night with them. I shouldn't worry myself about it if I were you, Lady Culwarren," observed Miss Paget, quietly.

"Not worry myself about it, Miss Paget? *Not worry*, when my only son has not slept in his bed all night, and may be lying murdered somewhere, for aught I know! But then, of course, you can't understand a mother's feelings. You don't know what it is to have brought a child into the world. How should you?"

"True, as you say, how should I? But then you were just as anxious last time Culwarren stayed out, you must remember, and he reminded you that he was a man, and capable of looking after himself. And he is right."

"I thank you, Miss Paget. I am much obliged to you for teaching me my duty," replied the Countess, in an offended tone. Miss Paget left her seat and approached the Countess's side.

"Don't be angry with me, my dear friend. I did not mean to offend you."

"But you *do* offend me. Everybody offends me. It is not likely you should observe Culwarren as I have done. He is totally different from what he has ever been before. He stays away at all times and evades the questions I put to him, looks wretchedly pale and ill, and can't eat his breakfast. If you knew anything about young men, you'd acknowledge he could not display worse symptoms."

"But of *what*?"

"Oh, of anxiety, suspense, disgust of everything

around him. I know perfectly well the reason of it all. It's Lily."

" I, Aunt Emily ? " cried the girl, starting.

"Certainly! *You!* If you would fulfil the promise you once made, you would win him back to his former self. My poor boy is not to blame. It is misery that has made him what he is. It is your unkindness that has wrought this sad change in him."

"Oh, Aunt Emily, indeed you are mistaken! My cousin and I have had several conversations on this subject, and he has no wish for me to feign an attachment I cannot feel. He knows I love him with a sister's love, and he is satisfied with that."

"It is not true," replied the Countess. "You are a disobedient and ungrateful girl, and have entirely misrepresented the matter. Of course, if you are unmaidenly enough to tell Culwarren that you are still hankering after that fellow, Anthony what's-his-name—for I'm sure I don't know what his name is——"

At this thrust Miss Paget's breast heaved with indignation.

"Don't you think," she said, with an immense effort, "that we might leave any reference to that unfortunate young man out of the discussion? He is gone from amongst us for ever. He is, as it were, dead to the family of Culwarren, and the dead should always be held sacred."

"I *must* allude to him, Miss Paget, if my niece compels me to do so. He refused her love before us all, and yet she still openly avows her devotion to him. She can have no pride left."

"Oh, Aunt Emily, you are cruel both to him and me," exclaimed Lily, as she threw herself into Miss Paget's arms. "You force me to tell you that it is because Anthony is nameless and outcast that I cannot forget him, and that there is nothing I cherish so much as the memory of his love for me."

"This is intolerable. It is positively indecent," cried Lady Culwarren, fanning herself more vigorously than ever. "No, don't cling to Miss Paget in that melodramatic manner. I am sure she would be the last person to encourage such boldness."

The companion pressed a kiss upon Lily's forehead, and then put her gently from her.

"Dear child," she said, softly, "you must learn to bear your troubles as we all do—alone."

"Well, really," cried the Countess, "one would think that to be asked to marry an earl was tantamount to going on the parish. If Miss Osprey intends to make so great a favour of it, I shall strongly advise my son to offer his coronet to some less particular young lady. But here is Culwarren himself. Now I suppose we shall have another scene."

The young Earl entered the apartment with rather a festive appearance, although he looked tired and sleepy. It was not the policy of his newly found friends to let him lose money at first, and he had begun to think himself even a cleverer fellow than before. It was not often, so they told him, that a man who could write novels and sonnets could also distinguish himself by winning so easily at pool and baccarat from old hands like themselves. So Lord Culwarren was becoming more intoxicated with his new pleasures and associates each day, and had already threatened his mother with taking up his quarters in another hotel if she continued to object to his hours of coming in and going out. He swaggered into the room on the present occasion, and having saluted the ladies, without a word of explanation took possession of an arm-chair.

"Just a cup of coffee, Miss Paget, if you please. Nothing more; I'm not hungry this morning."

"You never *are* hungry, Culwarren," observed the Countess, majestically. "You have lost your appetite completely since you came to this place. You will kill yourself if you go on at this rate."

"You wouldn't say so if you had seen me eating grilled bones and drinking champagne at four o'clock this morning, mother. A man can't be eating all day, you know."

"Four o'clock in the morning! What a disgraceful hour!" retorted Lady Culwarren. "And pray when did you return to the hotel?"

"About half an hour ago. Just had time to change my things. Fact is, I fell asleep on a sofa at my friends' place, and didn't wake till ten.

What time is it now ? " looking at his watch. "Ah, twelve! and," with a yawn, "what are we going to do this morning?"

" *We* are going to the Palazzo Farnese," replied his mother, severely. " I should think the best thing *you* could do would be to go to bed."

" Well, perhaps I will, or take a siesta in the balcony. English post in yet ? "

" There are no letters for you, Culwarren. Only *The Times* and *Morning Post*. But you have not yet told us with whom you dined last night."

" What can it signify to you ? " said Culwarren, as he opened the newspapers with a good deal of rustling. " You wouldn't recognise the names if I were to tell them to you."

" But I wish to know. You surely do not accept the hospitality of persons of whom you are ashamed."

" Certainly not. They are English gentlemen whom I met at the club here. But *you* are not likely to meet them."

" Why do you not bring them to the hotel to

be introduced to me? You always brought your friends to Gardenholme."

"That was different. But if you will receive these at Gardenholme with proper courtesy perhaps I may induce them to come," said the Earl, with a laugh.

"Culwarren, there is a mystery in all this that I cannot understand," persisted his mother. "Why should you be so unwilling to tell me with whom you pass your time? You absent yourself from our society almost every evening. You keep such hours as you never kept in your life before, and yet you are resolutely reticent concerning your friends, your amusements, and the places which you visit. Is this treating me with proper respect and confidence?"

"Perhaps not," replied the Earl, yawning; "but then you must remember we are no longer at Gardenholme. You have cooped me up there like a schoolboy, tied to your apron-string, for five-and-twenty years, but now I am a man, and I intend to see a little life. I have my reasons for the reticence you complain of. I don't wish to provoke any domestic quarrels or arguments, and probably were I to tell you the names of my chief friends in Florence, you would never leave off worrying me to give them up."

"You acknowledge, then, that they are not reputable acquaintances, Culwarren?"

"By no means, mother. But you would be likely to say so."

"I should think you might at all events give me the option."

"If you make a point of it, I will. But remember this, mother, I am not going to give up my friends, whatever you may think about them. I am my own master, and intend to do as I choose in all things for the future; and if, after having worried their names out of me, you begin to worry me about themselves, I shall take up my quarters in another hotel, and leave you ladies to keep each other company."

Lady Culwarren's curiosity was now fairly aroused. Who *could* these people be who, by their influence, had almost changed the nature of her son? She was determined to know.

"Of course, my dear boy," she commenced, " I am aware that you are of full age to look after yourself. Only, cannot you sympathise with a mother's feelings at being excluded from your confidence for the first time in your life? I have no wish to interfere with your pleasures. I only want to know the names of the friends who engross so much of your time."

"Very well, mother. If you insist, it shall be so," said Culwarren, with rather a defiant air. "The names of my two best friends in Florence—the friends whom I will not give up for you or anybody—are Anthony Melstrom and Oliver Fosbrooke. Now you have it." And he returned to the perusal of his papers.

The Countess turned pale beneath her rouge with annoyance, but was too much surprised by the announcement to find any immediate answer to his words. Her companion breathed harder than usual and pressed her hand upon her heart, as though to still its rapid motion. But Lily Osprey, with her face all aflame, sprang forward, eagerly exclaiming:

"Anthony in Florence, and you have seen him! Oh, Culwarren, is it possible?"

"Haven't I just answered the question, Lily? But you needn't excite yourself over it, for *you're* not likely to see him. I don't believe Tony would come near any of you to save his life."

"I should think not, indeed," interposed the Countess, who had found her tongue again. "He would hardly presume so far, after the way in which he spoke to me on leaving Gardenholme. Sit down in your seat again, Lily. If you have no shame left, I must have some for you. If your cousin chooses, out of the goodness of his heart, to recognise this unhappy young man, rest assured *you* will have no opportunity of doing so, for the first time he crosses my path I leave Florence at once. I cannot submit to a second edition of the humiliation I have already gone through." And gathering the folds of her *peignoir* around her ample person, Lady Culwarren rose from her seat and sailed from the apartment.

"I should think poor Tony might have echoed

that sentiment," observed the Earl, as he returned to the perusal of his papers.

"I'm afraid you have vexed your mother very much," said the companion, with a heavy sigh.

"I cannot help it, Miss Paget. Nothing has pleased me so much, since coming abroad, as meeting old Tony again. I shall never cease to regard him as a brother."

"Your feelings do you credit, Culwarren. And—how is he? He was my little pupil with yourself, you know, years ago," continued Miss Paget, with a sickly smile, "so I may be forgiven for being anxious to have news of his welfare."

"He seems jolly enough with his friend Fosbrooke, who is a regular brick," replied the Earl; "but he is very sore upon everything connected with the past, so that it is a tabooed subject between us. They spend the gayest life possible, and are out every night at theatres, casinos, or wine and card parties."

"Indeed! I hope Anthony will not be led into dissipation. And you, too, my dear Culwarren. Amuse yourself as much as you will, but be careful with whom you associate. These foreign societies are very mixed sometimes. And your mother has but one thought—for your welfare and happiness, so you must be patient with her."

"Oh, I'll take care of myself, Miss Paget, never fear," rejoined the Earl, carelessly; "and, indeed, with Anthony and Fosbrooke on either side of me, I don't see how I *can* go wrong."

"Come, Lily, then," continued the companion, rising, "let us go to our rooms and prepare to drive with Lady Culwarren."

But as soon as they were safe from observation, Lily clung about Miss Paget's neck and burst into tears.

"Oh, Miss Paget, Miss Paget, what *shall* I do? To know he is so near, and yet not to be able to see or speak to him. My poor Tony!"

The elder woman stroked the girl's hair very lovingly, and pressed the tear-stained face close to her heart.

"Dear Lily, is it not better so? What good could come of your meeting? It would only be useless pain for both."

" But I love him ! I love him ! "

" Hush, hush ! Try and cast the thought away from you as something sinful. You could never marry him, dear. It would be impossible."

" But *why* ? "

" You know well. Why make me reiterate the bitter truth ? Poor Anthony is a nameless man, without parents, family, or friends. He is no fit match for the niece of the Countess of Culwarren, and your aunt would never give her consent to such a marriage, which would reflect disgrace even upon your descendants."

" Then I shall never marry any one, Miss Paget, but remain single, like you."

" Dear child, perhaps you will be happier so. Marriage does not always confer happiness, Lily. We have but to look round on our married friends to see the truth of that."

" It would—with Anthony," whispered Lily.

" I thought we had agreed not to talk of that, my dear ? "

" What is the use of not speaking, when my

heart is full of nothing else? Day and night I think of him and pray for him, Miss Paget. The memory of that last terrible day, when Aunt Emily turned him out of the Abbey, is always present with me. I can hear his horror-stricken voice, can see the pain in his dear eyes. And what had he done wrong? Nothing—nothing! It was those who had placed him in such a position who were alone to blame. And even if my love can never do him any good, I will love him, and him only, till I die."

"My darling, *darling* child," said Miss Paget, kissing her fondly; and when Lily raised her head to return the loving embrace, she was surprised to see that the eyes of the usually placid and calm companion were brimming with tears.

"Ah! you have come to think differently about him since the time you spoke to me of this at Gardenholme, Miss Paget," she exclaimed. "You would not tell me *now* to marry my cousin Culwarren. You will not say that love is all a lie!"

"Indeed, Lily, you mistake me. I sympathise

with your attachment for Anthony, but I beg of you not to encourage it, or it may lose you all your present friends. The poor boy is too proud to ask you to be his wife. In cherishing his memory you are hugging a chimera to your breast. Far better to think of him as a dear, lost brother only. You heard what Culwarren said—that Anthony avoids even the mention of our names, so he must have abandoned all intentions with regard to you. And Culwarren is so good and amiable, Lily. How warmly and generously he speaks of poor Anthony ! That alone should make you love him and try to accede to his wishes."

"No, no, Miss Paget, it is impossible. My heart is fixed. At one time, when I had neither seen nor heard of Anthony for a year, I thought I might do as my aunt wished me, and sometimes I think that the terrible trouble that has overtaken me since is a punishment for my weakness then ; but from the moment I met Tony again the thought of marriage with Culwarren became a sacrilege—a blasphemy ! If I am not Tony's wife, I will be the wife of no one. If I may not love him openly, I will love him secretly until I die."

"May God bless you!" exclaimed Miss Paget, fervently, as she folded the girl in her arms.

END OF VOL. I.

LONDON: SPENCER BLACKETT, ST. BRIDE STREET, E.C.